THE SHERIFF OF TOMBSTONE

THE SHERIFF OF TOMBSTONE

TODHUNTER BALLARD

WHEELER
CHIVERS

This Large Print edition is published by Wheeler Publishing, Waterville, Maine, USA and by BBC Audiobooks Ltd, Bath, England.
Wheeler Publishing is an imprint of Thomson Gale, a part of The Thomson Corporation.
Wheeler is a trademark and used herein under license.

LIBRARY OF CONGRESS CATALOGING-IN-PUBLICATION DATA

Ballard, Todhunter, 1903–
   The sheriff of Tombstone / by Todhunter Ballard. — Large print ed.
   p. cm. — (Wheeler Publishing large print western)
   ISBN-13: 978-1-59722-513-7 (softcover : alk. paper)
   ISBN-10: 1-59722-513-4 (softcover : alk. paper)
   1. Large type books. I. Title.
PS3503.A5575S45 2007
813'.52—dc22
                                        2007002392

BRITISH LIBRARY CATALOGUING-IN-PUBLICATION DATA AVAILABLE

Published in 2007 in the U.S. by arrangement with
Golden West Literary Agency.
Published in 2007 in the U.K. by arrangement with
Golden West Literary Agency.

U.K. Hardcover: 978 1 405 64110 4 (Chivers Large Print)
U.K. Softcover: 978 1 405 64111 1 (Camden Large Print)

Printed in the United States of America on permanent paper
10 9 8 7 6 5 4 3 2 1

THE SHERIFF OF TOMBSTONE

CHAPTER 1

Riding down Arizona Territory's San Pedro Valley through the rich grama grass that tickled his big gray's belly John Savage had no prescience that in the next few hours the entire direction and thrust of his life would change again.

He had all he wanted here, had had for some years. The way had been long. A silent, private, seldom-smiling man, he was given to introspection, forever alert for a perspective on changing circumstances and how they should affect him and his.

He paused at the top of a knoll to look down on the deep, green meadow unfolded below, waving like water currents in the breeze. He rode like a trooper, ramrod straight, rather than with the rocking-chair flexibility of most ranch hands. He had been a trooper with the First Texas Horse and he had never changed the habit. His life had fallen into distinct patterns and he had accommodated his actions to fit them. It would take more than an average crisis to make him alter his mode of life another time.

As he watched the sinuous grasses he thought back through the years that had brought him to this point. He was not native to Arizona and was still somewhat bemused by the series of steps that had taken him to ownership of the widespreading Lazy S and his position as one of the foremost ranchers of the territory.

That he was here at all was attributable to a chain of coincidences of which he had taken advantage as they arose. He had been sixteen when he rode out with the Texas Horse to win a sergeant's stripes in the army of the new Confederacy. He had earned a battlefield commission as a second lieutenant to replace a close friend killed in action, a commission he had held until a Minié ball lodged in his leg and he was invalided home to west Texas.

Silently he swore at the old wound that still gave him pain as he put the gray at an easy jog off the knoll toward Tombstone. He gave a brief glance backward at the headquarters ranch he had built at the head of a draw so that its main gate fronted on Mexico, with the international line less than a mile south.

The present structure was not his first one here. When he had first trailed a full herd into the country, in 1865, he and his crew of over forty men had thrown up a temporary pole shanty with a grass roof and a dirt floor. It became a honeymoon shelter for himself and his bride of only weeks. The permanent buildings had been begun a year later, after he had established markets for his steers in booming Tombstone, at the San Carlos Indian Agency and with the construction camps of the Benson railroad crews. For the new ranch home he had hired a crew of Mexican laborers and sent them into the higher elevations to cut timber for the more elaborate headquarters buildings. The house was patterned after the one he had left in Texas, two squares connected by a trot through which the downdraft blew late every afternoon.

It was a good location, chosen with deliberate study, supplying water from an underground stream, feed for a large herd and shelter from the winter blasts that swept off the snow-topped Dragoons. Most winters were mild at this altitude and the breeze from the heights was cooling even in the hottest months.

He recalled arriving home in west Texas

fresh from the army hospital, barely able to hop on a homemade crutch. He had found that Comanches were raiding unchallenged, burning outlying ranches, murdering women and children and running off the horses and cattle. Most of the able-bodied Texas men were still fighting the tragic war.

As his leg healed he considered the situation, weighing it with a natural judgment of balances, deciding that he was more needed to fight Indians in Texas than by the army of the faltering Confederacy. When at length he could ride he joined the Rangers and fought with them until the war dragged to its close. Then he looked for a way to build a future.

The Southwest was in shambles. Hardly a man had a coin in his pockets. The ranches were burned, leaving blackened chimneys standing or in disrepair. Texas was prostrate. The only things of possible value left on the sweeping plains were cattle, and they were worth nothing locally.

There were many thousands of animals gone wild, some over twelve years old, never branded. In the country's disarray any unmarked animal belonged to the rider who could brute it out of the tangled thorn brush near the Gulf Coast and run an iron on it. Mavericking, they called it.

It was the only prospect with a glimmer of hope John Savage could see. He waited until Bo Roberts, his lifelong friend, wandered back to the area in rags of uniform, then set out with Bo and Old Sam, the black man the family had brought west from Louisiana when he and Savage were small boys, as near a brother as John Savage claimed, to try their luck with mavericking. A week of it was all John needed to decide there was no profit in that exercise.

Around their campfire Savage talked about the wide-horned, ferocious cattle that had fought them every inch and were dragged into the open only by combined attack. "They're too wild to handle this way. It would take two years to gather a herd worth driving to the railroad with only three of us hazing them. There's no way for us to haul them out of these thickets, brand, earmark, castrate and hold them in enough numbers without help."

"Where," Bo Roberts asked in sarcasm, "do we look for help?"

"I'll think on that."

John Savage thought on the problem all night. It was not that he was slow-witted, he was anything but that, but his whole instinct and training was in caution. In the army and on the frontier a man who went off half-cocked could be dead before he realized he had made a mistake. In the morning, while the black man boiled parched corn that substituted as coffee and soaked strips of dried beef that even cooked were almost too tough to chew, while Bo Roberts mended his lariat that the thorns had snagged and raveled, Savage outlined a possible way of recruiting a crew.

"The country is crawling with brush jumpers doing just what we've tried and they're having no better luck. They can round up one or two hundred head but that's nowhere near enough to make a drive pay out. But if enough of us throw in together we can make up a herd."

Neither Roberts nor Sam commented, long accustomed to the Colonel's thinking aloud and knowing he did not like interruption. Of course Savage was not a colonel, had never been more than a brevetted lieutenant, but Sam had promoted him when he came home and Bo accepted the title as a joke when there was little to laugh at. At first Savage had protested in irritation. He had never laid claim to anything to which he was not entitled, but while he healed, while he rode with the Rangers, he discovered that so many returning veterans were upgrading their rank that soon Texas counted more "colonels" than even Kentucky and he quit arguing. Now it even began to pay off.

At the first maverickers' camp they approached there were three young men, half-starved, narrow-headed, suspicious. They had combed out nearly two hundred longhorns in a rough log corral and both animals and riders viewed the new arrivals with equal hostility.

John Savage did not blame the beaten soldiers. As if the state had not suffered enough these last years Texas was now strangled by carpetbaggers, human vultures from the North who had swept down through the conquered land, welcomed by the newly freed blacks while the whites were disenfranchised for their allegiance to the Confederacy. These boys, seeing Sam riding at Savage's side, took the visitors to be such adventurers as were inventing new taxes, here to grab their scrawny cattle. But in that empty territory there were amenities to observe. Savage and Bo were invited to light a spell and the Colonel beckoned Old Sam down.

Savage was not at all sure he could talk these wary three into joining forces under the circumstances. One was wearing the blouse of a Confederate uniform but neither

John nor Bo had on anything gray and Savage resolved that both would break out their rebel jackets when they called on the other camps to thaw the icy reception. He badly wanted this gather to add to his, but they shook their heads at the proposition.

Until one who had not taken his eyes off Savage's face said uncertainly, "Weren't you a lieutenant at Vicksburg? You look familiar."

Savage used a rare smile. "Sure I was. With the First Texas Horse. Should I know you?"

The nearly vacant eyes changed, brightened a bit. The man spat into the small dung fire. "Doubt you'd recall. I was orderly for the field hospital. You were out of your head when they brought you in. I helped bring you out of the wagon and you fought me like hell. I didn't forget your face. I don't forget many."

Everybody relaxed. They said they were brothers from around Austin, planning to push a few steers north where rumor hinted there was a market of sorts, and they were now ready to listen to the rest of Savage's pitch. They hadn't really paid attention to him earlier.

He repeated what he had said and embellished the story. As nearly as he could make out, Baxter Springs was about fifteen hundred miles north; from what scratchy information he had accumulated that was the closest shipping point.

Cows were worthless here in the South. Even the old hide and tallow buyers around Galveston, who were the market for the early Texas herders, were gone and bankrupt. What capital they had was in Confederate paper. For emphasis Savage told of a cattle buyer coming back from New Orleans with a trunkful of such notes who finally burned them because no one would accept them.

"The way it was told to me," he said, "these animals will bring twelve to fifteen Yankee dollars in Kansas at the railhead. That kind of money is a lot these days. Your families could eat on it. But we have to get them there, a long way up through the Nations, and nothing under two thousand head would be worth the drive."

They stirred dejectedly. It would take months to capture and brand so many. The Colonel let them sweat for a long moment, then went on.

"None of us could do it alone, but if we combine your gather and ours and whatever the other boys have, join up to make as big a crew as possible for safe passage through the Indian Territory, we can all benefit. It won't be easy, but nothing worth having is."

"With everything mixed in together how do we tell which animal is whose?"

"Each of us trail-brands his own bunch before we make up the herd and we can cut them out at the railroad."

That satisfied the Ballou brothers, even enthused them where there had been hardly a spark of hope before. Savage, Bo Roberts and Sam helped to road-mark the Ballous' two hundred head, then rode on looking for other camps. The Ballous would move their animals, pick up Savage's and hold both herds a few miles out of Austin to wait for more. The idea took hold. From the nucleus of maverickers Savage talked to, word of the plan filtered farther afield. When they were all ready to drive there were over twenty-five hundred steers and forty-three riders to push them.

Looking back on it now as he made his way to Tombstone, Savage wondered if he would have the brashness to tackle such an ordeal again, especially if he had known the obstacles in the way. But he was young, the men with him were young and all were hungry. Hunger did a lot to make risks worth taking.

The road up through the Nations was well established. Half the Americans who had drifted into the territory had followed it into Texas, crossing the Red River into the Nations at Colbert's Ferry, just north of Preston, Texas. But those early immigrants had come in wagons and buckboards and what they had needed was little help to a cattle train. The trace had kept close to timber for wood to cook over, for repairing broken wheels and wagons. Timber was the last thing the ragged boys shoving the big herd north wanted. It was hard enough controlling the wild, heavy brutes without having to stop every mile to comb them out of trees and brush.

And timber was only their initial travail. Working slowly north past Boggy Depot to Tahlequah, capital of the Cherokee Nation, they followed the route to Marysville, Arkansas, through Springfield, Missouri, but instead of keeping to it into St. Louis they cut off toward Baxter Springs. Every mile of that first drive was still vivid to John Savage. Besides fighting timber they ran into Indians as they crossed their territory. The red men demanded a tribute of a hundred steers for allowing them to pass.

In spite of the outrage of the riders Savage gave up the longhorns as a reasonable price for the many miles to be saved. But when the lumbering column was stopped a second time within twenty miles and another hundred beasts asked for Savage refused, ordering the red men to clear the way. Instead, this band of perhaps a hundred tried to stampede the whole herd, firing rifles in the air and howling, racing their ponies down the line of easily terrified cattle.

Savage wheeled and drove after them, leveling his rifle, and shot the leader off his pony. That ended the shakedown attempt. The Indian had been a popular subchief and his band suddenly lost their taste for the beeves.

That shot cemented the crew into a unit. Until then a number of the other owners had argued his authority over them. Thereafter they paid him a growing respect. It came at an important time, for more problems lay ahead.

The first warning of further difficulty surfaced ten miles short of Baxter Springs. Savage was riding point when a dust cloud was kicked up by a dozen riders running their mounts toward the herd. Savage lifted an arm, signaling that the herd be stopped, and walked his horse out with his rifle in the crook of his arm. The newcomers also pulled up except for one who came on to confront Savage with a hangdog question.

"Where you fellows headed?"

"Railroad. Where else?"

Savage sized up the man, gaunt beneath the stubble of beard that straggled over hollow cheeks, wearing much-patched overalls and the remnants of a Confederate major's uniform. A bony man who wagged his head dolefully.

"You won't get there, mister."

"Why not?"

"Why not?" The words dripped bitterness. "Because there's a slew of nesters, Quantrill guerrillas and northern jayhawkers ahead who rode with Lane. They've got a blockade. They claim Texas cattle bring in ticks and the ticks give the local stock Texas fever."

"That true?"

"How the hell do I know?" The man scratched at his whiskers with a grimy claw. "Whether or no, they took our cows, shut them in a holding corral and grabbed our guns, told us to high-tail it back down the trail. We asked for food and the bastards laughed. Said the more Texans who starved the better."

"Damnyankees," Savage commiserated. "I'm John Savage."

"Lew Trumble."

"What outfit?"

"Second Louisiana Dragoons." The voice

19

was acid. "We lose the war, the carpetbaggers steal everything down home and now after we sweat over three months making a gather, that's stolen too. What's a man to do?"

Savage's lip curled. "Just drift back south with your tails curled under like yellow pups? No wonder the war was lost."

The major flushed but his tone turned ragged with temper. "Big talk. What better do you think you can do?"

"What I started out for." Savage showed no anger, kept his words flat, unequivocal. "Push this herd to the rails and sell them."

Trumble was scornful. "Just get everybody killed is what. That crowd around Baxter is tough. Most of them were murderers while they rode around playing soldier."

Unimpressed, Savage said evenly, "We can shoot as well as they can. And you ought to be able to. Turn around. Join us and we'll get your critters back. How many men have they?"

"Lots more than you and us together." But there was a hint of renewed hope in the dark, tortured eyes.

As usual John Savage studied his options for some time, then waved all the men to him and laid out a plan of action. When the major's group was rearmed Savage split the enlarged crew into two forces. The larger number, his own men, he left under his trail boss, Bo Roberts, with Sam as aide, their orders to continue north slowly, not to run tallow off the animals. Along with Sam, Savage and Roberts had grown up together on neighboring ranches. The two white boys had joined the Texas Horse at the same time and when Savage was wounded it was Roberts who had carried him to the dressing station.

Savage took with him the smaller detail, half of Trumble's people, and because he wasn't certain they would stand in a showdown he added twelve from his own crew. They set out toward the confiscated gather at a deliberate pace to keep their horses fresh, camped a mile short of the corral for the night and fed the new contingent their first food of the day.

Just at the following sunrise they hit the corral that Trumble had said was guarded by some twenty nesters. The guards did not expect attack and most were asleep. The force with Savage was so small that it raised hardly any dust as they approached. The Colonel stretched them in a skirmish line and drove forward from three sides.

The sun, just above the horizon, blinded the guards as they waked to the warning shouts of the sentries on watch. Unable to count how many were outside the fence, they reacted in panic. They were soon ringed by a circle of leveled rifles and disarmed without firing a shot. While their arms were collected Savage had them lined up against the corral poles and read them a short warning.

"Light out of this country and stay out. If we ever see any of you again we'll shoot you on the spot."

His steady, cold eyes held them. They had been guerrillas, by nature violent men, and they recognized the potential violence in Savage and believed his warning. They left in sullen haste.

Savage kept Trumble's steers corralled where they were to wait for Bo Roberts and the main herd. He posted lookouts for all four directions in case others from Baxter Springs came out to retake the cattle. Taking turns, they breakfasted on the food the guerrillas had left behind.

Before long one of the lookouts called an alert and Savage went to see what was approaching. A small plume of dust on the road indicated that there must be only a single rider. Savage lined his men up with cocked rifles, then with his own long gun swinging from one hand, he walked out to receive the newcomer.

The man hauled up within comfortable speaking distance and sat easy. He was as young as Savage, a lank figure, a towhead whose hair curled from under his hard hat, falling to his shoulders. He did not appear hostile. His clothes suggested a city resident. Instead of regular cowboy dress or the buckskin of buffalo hunters he wore a black wool suit, pants tucked into boots, a frock coat and derby. He crossed his hands on his saddle horn and smiled down through light blue eyes.

"Name's Joe McCoy, from Springfield." The tone was mild and sounded as if he half expected the name to be recognized.

The Colonel shook his head. "Savage, west Texas." He waited for more information.

McCoy tipped the derby back with a forefinger and used a white handkerchief to wipe over his face and neck. "Going to be another hot one, friend. What have you got in mind for this jag of cattle?"

"Sell them at the railroad." Savage's tone was neutral.

"In Baxter?" McCoy cawed a laugh. "Not a chance. There are enough farmers and fighters in these parts to wipe you out."

"Maybe. I have a good crew on the way

with our main herd. Over fifty riders and they've all been fighting a long while."

"Still not enough guns. How big is the herd all told?"

"Close to twenty-five hundred. A combine the crew and I put together."

McCoy smiled again, took time to roll a cigarette, then flipped the makings down to Savage before he spoke again.

Through his first exhalation he said unhurriedly, "Could be we can do each other some good. Savage, the Kansas Pacific won't touch your animals because of ticks. Same with the Missouri Pacific. The farmers would boycott them if they did, and the roads live off their shipments."

Savage tensed. It had not occurred to him that any railroad would refuse his beef. His mouth widened in a straight line of determination.

"I'll ship. If I have to drive clear to St. Louis."

"Not possible either. The whole way is thick with jayhawkers and guerrillas. Your only answer is to turn west."

"Oh? How far to the nearest railhead?"

"Doesn't matter. Salina is no better than Baxter. But" — the young man had an infectious grin and waggled his fingers — "closer, east of Salina, there's a whistle stop with a water tank, a woodpile and nothing else in the middle of miles of empty prairie. I worked a deal with a jerk line called the Hannibal and St. Jo and got a concession from the K.P. They'll put in a siding at the place . . . called Abilene . . . where the Hannibal, St. Jo will pick up steers for me and haul them to Chicago. Bypass St. Louis altogether."

Savage asked in suspicion, "A tank and a woodpile is all? How do you get cattle into the cars? They don't fly."

"We can build stock pens and loading chutes when we get there, while the spur's being laid down. You say the word and I'll wait for your herd and lead you to Abilene. A little while and she'll be the biggest shipping point in Kansas."

So it was that John Savage became the first drover to push longhorns to Abilene. While the crew put up the facilities, the animals fattened themselves. During the rest the animals gained more weight than they had carried when they had been dragged fighting and bellowing out of the thorn brush. McCoy paid twelve dollars a head and the crew lingered to see the cars filled and to watch the train pull away without interference.

That first year the young promoter's boast

of Abilene's growth fell far short of his hopes. Tales of nester troubles filtered south before word of the new shipping center. Only some thirty-five thousand animals were loaded at the tank stop. But the Hannibal and St. Jo hauled those to Illinois, keeping well away from the dangerous stretch to St. Louis, and so established Chicago as what would become the greatest meat-packing city in the country.

After that first successful venture up the trail John Savage changed from prewar rancher to drover. Most of his original combine members stayed with him as hired hands and his second herd was as large as others. That season a quarter of a million animals lumbered up the long, trying miles, this time traveling the Chisholm Trail, the road the government had paid the half-breed Jesse Chisholm to lay out for moving the Indian population from the vicinity of Wichita to the new reservation in Indian Territory.

Savage used it and in later years took the newer western route, the Fort Dodge Trail. He tried the track carved out by Oliver Loving and Charles Goodnight, starting at San Angelo in west Texas, running west to strike the Pecos River at Horsehead Crossing and following up the waterway to Fort Sumner,

New Mexico. That was the least favored way because of a ninety-mile stretch without water, but other than that the little traffic it carried left more grass for late-starting herds.

The Loving-Goodnight Trail had another advantage for John Savage. It led directly to Las Vegas, New Mexico, a settlement that had developed into the major supply point for growing Denver and the proliferating mining camps in the high Colorado mountains. Here was a hungry market and there was no middle man or shipping costs to cut into Savage's profits. On that drive a series of circumstances arose that would again drastically change the direction of his life.

When he and his crew reached Las Vegas and the herd was tallied, five hundred head were missing. It was not unusual. Any time a drover pushed through settled ranch country a few of his stragglers would drift off among the local cattle. Most herders discounted the shortages rather than lose time rounding them up. Not John Savage. He had brought those animals a long way, they represented a good deal of money at the rising market price and he meant to have them all back.

He sold what animals had arrived to the

27

Doyle Company, paid his crew and sent most of them back to west Texas, keeping with him only Bo Roberts and Old Sam, then the three set out backtracking their trail to cut every herd they had passed. Neither the foreman nor Sam approved, knowing that once a stray had joined a rancher's herd the rancher would fight to keep the animal. Sure enough, at their first stop trouble found them.

It was on John Chisum's vast spread close to Bosque Grande. Chisum was one of the most powerful men in New Mexico, controlling thousands of acres and half a million cattle, but that did not mean he would not welcome a few more free head.

All three men knew this, knew Chisum's reputation, but obedient to Savage's order Roberts and Sam joined him. They had combed out sixty steers wearing the Lazy S brand when Roberts pointed across the range. A streak of dust followed hard-riding horsemen at a run toward them.

Bo Roberts said in a nervous, quiet voice, "Hope that's not who I'm afraid it is. I hear old Chisum is a mean bugger, he'd as soon shoot you as not."

The black man made no comment but his eyes rolled white in agreement.

Savage said only, "Keep them moving, Bo,

and Sam, watch my back." He sat quiet, awaiting the new arrivals, his side arm drawn.

There were five, Chisum and four of his crew. The rancher drove in and pulled up his mount so hard it nearly went back on its haunches. Chisum's big face was angry red under his heavy tan, a vein in his temple visibly throbbing.

"What the hell you think you're doing with my cattle?" he bawled.

Savage's voice was clear, carrying but level. "Taking back those wearing my Lazy S."

"No you ain't. It's been vented."

"By whom?"

"By me." Chisum continued roaring, fishing a folded paper from a pocket and shaking it at Savage.

The Colonel did not reach for it, but unhurriedly lifted the gun and steadied its aim on Chisum's head. The rancher's riders had fanned out and drawn but Savage knew without looking that Sam had his rifle ready and could use it expertly. Roberts was busy quieting the gather made restless by the shouting.

Still evenly, pleasantly, Savage said, "Looks like you reached for the bargain of the year, Mr. Chisum."

The man's brows climbed. "I don't know you. You know me?"

"Certainly. It's my custom to know who a rancher is before I cut out my cows from his."

The voice and the gun were steady. The confrontation lengthened into a stare-down contest. Chisum was not used to being challenged by anyone. He had no idea of the identity of the man facing him and, although he had four men to back him, instinct warned that he might himself be killed if the face-down wasn't broken quickly. His own eyes fell but he still roared.

"I ain't got time to haggle over a little clutch of scrawny critters. Get them off my land and you keep off."

He swung an arm, wheeled his big horse and spurred away, his men following agape. They had never before seen their boss backed down.

CHAPTER 2

At that time John Savage had no intention of settling anywhere, least of all in Arizona Territory, which he had never seen. He loved the freedom of the drover's life and the slow daily changes of the geographical scene. Trail driving could be hard work but it was largely leisurely. Cattle pushed too fast lost weight and therefore value, and they needed a good deal of time to graze. He liked traveling with his crew, the only people for whom he felt friendship, and he saw no reason not to continue moving around.

When he and Roberts and Sam finished picking up his strays they had almost the whole five hundred head again. There were not enough of the salvaged animals to make a return to Las Vegas pay and taking them back to Texas made no sense. Bo Roberts suggested they swing over to Tombstone, which was just commencing to boom as a silver-mining center.

"I been hankering for a look at one of them mining camps and that's closer than anyplace we can sell this little bunch," he said with a touch of wistfulness.

Tombstone might be closest but it was still a long drag. John Savage had no interest in silver mining or any other kind. The underground was no place he wanted to go, but such places did offer a market, a good one. Through Las Vegas he had supplied a lot of beef to the Colorado mountain towns. Why not try a shot at Tombstone? If it proved out he could make a double drive the following season, half for Las Vegas, the rest for Arizona, and even if that looked not to be worthwhile this was a chance to see some new country.

So they started for the San Pedro Valley. Before they reached the dry white sands they stopped at Tularosa to rest the herd for the savage ninety-mile drive across the barren desert, and it was at Tularosa that Savage found her.

He had been married once, at sixteen, the day before he and Bo went off to war, but his wife had died in a Comanche raid while he was fighting in Mississippi. It had been a hasty, war-triggered romance more than a deep love, but the death left a mark. When he began driving cattle he had vowed that if he ever did fall in love and marry again he would not leave the woman for any extended length of time. He would give up the trails and establish a home.

Edna Hannah was totally different from his diminutive west Texas wife. She was almost as tall as Savage, with a round face and orientally high cheekbones, dressed in trousers and a cotton shirt that stretched taut over her large, firm breasts. She was sitting on the top rail of a pole corral that held a few unexceptional-looking horses when Savage passed on the trail moving his animals toward the waterhole half a mile beyond. He stopped abruptly and sat admiring her. He saw her before she noticed him. Her rapt attention was on the passing steers, her gaze following the bunch, and she did not look toward Savage until he rode to her and spoke.

"Seems to me you like cattle, ma'am."

She started at the voice, turned, nodded and measured him with level, direct gray eyes, unsmiling. "I do. We have a few, nothing like as many as this herd."

Savage looked after the retreating rumps. He did not consider them a herd, only a jag. "Would your man want to buy these?" He had a flashing thought that if he could sell here in Tularosa it would save crossing the arid stretch where he expected to lose a number.

She showed surprise, then a slow smile came, a good, full, open show of humor. "My only men are my father and brothers. And we don't have that kind of money, Mr. . . ."

"Savage. John Savage. This your place?"

"For the time being. We move pretty often. I'm Edna Hannah, quarter Cherokee, born in Indian Territory."

She said it as naturally as if she had said she was part Scotch. Most breeds he had come across tried to disclaim their tribal blood, but this girl spoke with pride and gave him a steady inspection without hostility. He returned her smile warmly.

"Do you like moving around?"

"We seem to have to. Pa wasn't doing well back home, kept changing jobs, and when he heard about the silver strike over the mountains he loaded up and we started for it. But the horses aren't too good. They about played out when we got this far, then the liveryman warned us about the white sands, so here we sit."

There was no frustration in her tone, but John Savage had a sensitive perception and he read a fatalistic acceptance of her situation underlaid by a strong need for something better than this plight. His impulse was to make an immediate offer but even now he held back, considering.

"Would you like to come down to our camp for a while and watch the steers? I haven't talked with a lady for months."

"I'd love it." She dropped easily off the rail. "I'm lonesome too. Nobody around here likes Indians much."

The height of cowman gallantry was to give anyone his saddle and walk in high-heeled boots for half a mile. She tried to refuse his horse but Savage argued that it would not look right for him to ride beside her on foot.

They spent the full afternoon together. By sundown John Savage was totally committed and made a blunt proposal of marriage, and without coquetry she accepted. He had made his plans while they talked. He would take his gather on to Arizona and look for a good place to build. There would be one last ride to Texas to pick up his breeder herd. On his return he'd come through Tularosa, pick up her family and drive to wherever they would establish their ranch. It would be outside Texas, away from the ruined South. At dusk he saw her home, riding a remuda horse. He met her parents and brothers but paid them scant attention. His eyes were on her alone. It was the first time he had neglected to study all aspects of what he would do.

Savage hated parting from her when she came down to see them off at dusk four days later. He had bought a freight wagon and filled it with water barrels for the ninety-mile dry stretch. He planned to move through the cooler nights only, even though it was harder shoving the cattle during the hours they normally slept.

They lost six animals in the desert before winding through the Stein's Pass Mountains into the San Simon Valley. They then rounded the Chiricahuas and continued into the Sulphur Springs Valley. The Dragoons rose ahead, bare, bleak ridges of boulders and caves like the long skeleton of some giant prehistoric reptile. And just beyond them lay Tombstone.

All the way, as he passed through the territory, Savage felt the wide sweep of Arizona. The views took his breath and what he saw moved him strongly. He had never felt so about Texas, nor the Nations nor the Kansas frontier.

This was an ancient land, a place that had once lain beneath the sea, where marine shells enriched the sands, showing in abundance wherever water had worn a course and left cutbanks. Long ago, after the sea had receded, cave dwellers had built on the rocky mountain shelves, and ruins still stood sheltered in the shallow caves of Canyon Diablo and other cliffs. Later the Spaniards had terrorized the Indians in their greedy search for gold and silver and empire. For centuries the great valleys, running like fingers north and south from the stark mountains, had offered lavish and ideal graze for buffalo. Now the vast herds were gone, reduced by the white hunters to a point of near extinction, but the pasture-land remained, lush with rich grama grass that stood three feet and taller, and the long blue-stem was nearly as high.

Riding drag, Savage called to Bo Roberts and Sam ahead, patrolling both sides of the gather to keep it grouped. "Did either of you ever dream there was anything like this in the country?"

Sam wagged his head in awesome agreement. Bo Roberts was not an emotional man but even he was deeply impressed.

"This has everything a man could want," he called back. "The quicker we can find a spot and bring in the herd the better I'll like it."

They made more haste into Tombstone,

eager now to be rid of the plodding cattle. After selling the jag and the wagon, they spent two weeks in the San Pedro searching for just the right combination of pasture, water, climate and view. They found an ideal location and Savage staked his claim. A drover at heart, he regretted giving up the trails, but if he married he must, and Edna Hannah had become more important than driving cattle, and nowhere he might settle could compare with this.

The following spring he lined out his big breeding herd on the long trek to return to the San Pedro. With his entire crew to guard the animals they skirmished with Indians again, trailed across the Llano Estacado and climbed through the Sacramento Mountains to Tularosa again. There they laid over to rest the animals and to put the Hannah Conestoga in shape. And for John Savage to marry Edna.

He did not approach this union as a young romantic but with a serene confidence that they were well mated. A man who kept his long-range intentions to himself, he had not told his crew of his engagement until he had seen the girl again and been reassured that she had not changed her mind. The simple ceremony in the little church took them all by surprise.

When they did start into the white sands, the Conestoga carrying the Hannah household goods, with Savage driving, took the head of the long column with the water wagons next. The herds would move better if they could catch a scent of moisture in the air ahead.

He soon discovered the ineptitudes and weaknesses of his father-in-law, though he liked Edna's part-Cherokee mother. His opinions of the brothers were reserved until they could prove themselves.

The desert crossing was made with little loss and they had no problems until they reached the Rio Grande. Ordinarily the river was wide, placid, shallow enough to wade, but they found its banks full with spring runoff, a muddy, roiling current sluicing trees and bushes from the mountains above. Other men might have camped and waited for the flood to pass, but John Savage had crossed wild streams before and he was not about to sit cooling his heels and wasting time.

Charles Hannah, his wife's father, was driving their wagon that day while Savage rode his horse beside it. The four-horse team dragged it as far as the bank, then refused to enter the water. Hannah yelled at them, cracked his long whip against the rumps of the wheel animals, then sat back helplessly, shrugging.

John Savage hid his disgust. Even the horses found the driver wanting, the uncertainty of the man in some manner being translated to them. Savage spoke from his saddle.

"Can you swim?" He could have delegated one of his crew to what must be done but he intended that Hannah should pull his own weight in some part.

The man brightened eagerly. He was shamed at failing to control the team as he had been shamed at a long series of failures, but he had always been a strong swimmer and scrambled down from the high seat to prove he could do at least one thing well.

Old Sam had no peers at managing teams and Savage called on him. "Give him your saddle, Sam, and you take over the wagon. Hannah, get up, take hold of the off leader's head gear and pull him in. I'll handle the other side."

With Sam laying on the whip and Savage and Hannah dragging at the lead horses the animals surrendered and stepped warily into the swirling flood. Sam angled them upstream but the team was soon out of its depth, carried off its feet and forced to swim. The wagon, sunk to its bed, swung with the current and the team was barely able to tow it across a hundred yards downstream. At length they found footing and lurched up to dry land, Sam keeping them moving until the wagon wheels cleared the mud before he hauled them up to stand trembling and blowing.

While the Hannahs unloaded and spread those articles that had been soaked to dry, John Savage and the crew emptied the few barrels that still held water, crossed more easily with the lightened freighters, then began shoving the herd over. It took the rest of the day and the following morning, half the men camping on one side, half holding the remaining stock on the other shore overnight. They lost a few head that could not avoid the floating trees that swept down over them, but not too many. Savage laid over for the afternoon and night to let the frightened steers calm down and the crew dry out, and the following morning set out for Sulphur Springs Valley and the San Pedro beyond, where he had established his claim.

Reaching it, they threw the breeding stock onto the rich grass. Savage sent Bo Roberts with half the crew on to Tombstone and the Indian reservation to sell some of the herd. The rest of the hands he kept to put up pole shacks for shelter until there was time and money to build for permanence. It delighted him to watch his new wife's enthusiasm for the spot he had chosen.

The years had been successful far beyond any dreams of the young man who had put together that first combined herd in poverty-stricken Texas, though they had not been any easier than that first drive. Most of John Savage's San Pedro neighbors were outlaws. The Clantons, Curly Bill Brocious and his lieutenant, John Ringo, were the worst of the lot, though the valleys around Tombstone crawled with killers, stage robbers to whom anything they could steal was fair prize, rustlers and bandits raiding from Mexico. Even Sheriff John Behan was suspect. Rather than curtailing the criminals, he associated with them, even deputizing them on occasion.

Savage had fought off the first attack on his cattle and ridden to Tombstone to report to Behan that Ike Clanton had brought his gang, shouting who he was and that they would be back to burn Savage out. As usual Behan had not gone out against them.

Immediately afterward the Hannahs had moved to town, urging Edna to go with them; they claimed she would be safer there, but she would not leave. Savage set the family up in a small store and their older son stayed with them, but the other soon drifted on.

On a second attempt at the ranch Brocious' crowd joined the Clantons and made off with a hundred head of the Lazy S breeding stock. Savage did not again go to Behan. He took his crew, caught seven of the outlaws in a saloon at Galeyville, hanged them to a clump of cottonwoods and rounded up the stolen animals from the range Clanton claimed as his. A shock wave spread through the territory. The Arizona raiders were not accustomed to being challenged. They sent word that they still meant to burn the Lazy S and run off the whole herd. People in Tombstone rode out to warn Savage and were merely stared down by his cold eyes.

When the outlaws swarmed in on a third try they left a significant number of their party dead beyond the corral fence. No one ever came against the Lazy S again.

CHAPTER 3

Though the Savages had remained child-less, the Lazy S had prospered in the twelve years since its establishment. The mining camp of Tombstone had not. Three years before this day when John Savage rode toward the town for a meeting with Major Sawyer, the purchasing agent for the San Carlos Indian reservation, the silver boom had been at its peak. Tombstone had had a population of better than thirty-five thousand, over a hundred saloons and gambling clubs, a dozen hotels and whore parlors too numerous to count. A large segment of men had brought their families to settle along the hot and dusty side streets that ran off the main thoroughfares Tough Nut and Allen. Lew Trumble, one of the Texans whose small herd Savage and his crew had recaptured from the Baxter Springs nesters and guerrillas, and who had come to Arizona with the Colonel, had married one of the settlers' daughters, moved to town and entered its politics.

Then in a very short time the rich mines had flooded. An enormous underground water table had been tapped, and no pumps then available could draw off enough water to prevent the shafts and tunnels from filling. The bust came quickly, the population shrinking to less than three thousand in the next three years. Most of the stores and the saloons that had flourished around the clock held only grit on their shelves and the departed owners had not even bothered to lock their doors.

John Savage had watched the camp fail without personal regret. He had never had any particular need of it except as a market, and the Indian reservation and the railroad construction settlements had taken up the slack. He felt about it as he had felt about the Kansas cow towns. They had served a purpose but he had heartily disliked them. Tombstone was through, but as one newspaperman said as he shut down his print shop, left the door swinging open and loaded his hand press in the boot of a westbound stage, the camp was too tough to die entirely.

Savage scorned the straggle of loafers along Tough Nut as he passed. They were no part of his world. His focus was on his ranch in the lush San Pedro Valley.

At the O.K. Corral he swung down in the square of sunbaked earth that had been the scene of a multiple shootout, resulting in Wyatt Earp and his brothers being driven out of the territory. Savage had known the Earps casually and been ambivalent about them. He had taken no side in the long, fractious struggle between their faction and the outlaws Johnny Behan befriended. Many contended that the Earps had right on their side, but in John Savage's book they were damnyankees to be steered clear of.

He left his deep-chested gray in the enclosure and walked back to the Oriental, one of the few gambling saloons that remained in business. Today the heat on the gritty street drove idlers indoors, yet there were only six men in the long room when Savage shouldered through the batwings. Four played listless cards at a table. The two lounging at the bar edged away from the man they knew as hostile and taciturn. Savage knew none of their names but he knew the breed and despised them.

He bought a beer while he waited for the reservation agent, passed the time of day with the bartender, then dropped his eyes to the mug to discourage further conversation. He heard the hinges creak and the louvers flap open again and glanced at the backbar mirror, expecting to see the major. Instead it was Lew Trumble, the Texan who had left his crew soon after Savage settled on the San Pedro. Trumble paused to accustom his eyes to the dim interior after the glare of the street, then came toward Savage, his face solemn.

"Howdy, Colonel, I saw you come in and you're just the man I want to see."

Still looking in the mirror, now at Trumble's reflection, Savage said without curiosity, "Buy you a beer, Lew? What's on your mind?"

"A cold one sounds fine, thanks. I'm head of the county commission, you know, and I've just come from a meeting. They want to talk to you."

"I wouldn't know what for, I don't have any county problems."

Trumble drank his full mug at one lift and shoved it across the counter for a refill, dabbing foam from his lips with a handkerchief.

"You know much about what's going on in town? In all Cochise County for that matter?"

"I don't pay much attention. Hear the boys gossiping that the rowdies are acting up. Is there something else?"

"A whole lot else." Trumble's tone was

low, for Savage alone. "You know how in the boom days we had a lot of grief with the Clantons and such, and stage robberies, murdering Mexican smugglers, whole herds run off, but that's over. Now with the big money gone we've got cheap housebreakers and petty thieves holding up people for a couple of dollars every night. Hell, no one ever locked their doors until now, but it's got so we're broken in on regularly, anything that can be sold stolen night and day. We need your help. The commission wants you for sheriff."

The Colonel drained his glass to cover his astonishment and beckoned for refills. When the bartender moved off again he looked away from the mirror, faced Trumble directly.

"Thought you had a sheriff. What happened to Franklin?"

"Yesterday he hopped the train at Benson for Tucson and if I know weak-kneed Willie he won't stop this side of California. John, you're our only hope."

"Not interested, Lew. The Lazy S keeps me busy. This town is on its last legs and if people are smart they'll pack up and leave. With the mines shut down what is there to stay for?"

"We're stuck here, everything we have is

tied up in the town and county. It just has to be cleaned up. Listen to this, you've seen Chum's daughter Betsey around haven't you?"

"Pretty little sixteen-year-old girl."

"Yesterday she was yanked off the street on her way to a store, into an empty shop, and gang-raped."

Savage had just lifted his mug to his lips. He set it down hard. "Who did it?"

"If we knew they'd be swinging before now. That's why Franklin scooted when we pressured him to find out."

"Is Betsey badly hurt?"

"Still in shock. Doc Combs can't say when she'll come out of it or if she will. She just keeps whispering, 'So many times, so many times,' over and over. Colonel, you can't refuse to do your part in any conscience."

John Savage considered the prospect with bleak distaste. For one thing, if he gave in to Trumble he and Edna would have to leave the San Pedro and move to this sorry remnant of a town for his duration in office. For another, there was no one here they could call friends. Then there was the old antipathy of the southern cowmen who had driven herds to the railheads for the northern sheriffs and marshals who policed the towns and gave hard times to the trail-weary cowboys when they overcelebrated at the end of a drive. The law officer was the common enemy of the cattleman.

"You're a Texan," he said sourly. "You came up the trails with my crews. You know they'd disown me if I pinned on a badge. Then who'd run my ranch?"

But Trumble was dogged. "Who else could we turn to? You beat the early outlaws where nobody else could, and no one else can now. This country's been mighty good to you, given you high-paying markets for your beef for years. We think you owe it something back. At least come and talk to the commissioners. Or does the job scare you?"

"You know better."

Lew Trumble's shrewd thrust rankled Savage. With a heavy sigh and a weary shrug he stood up, scattered silver on the counter and told the bartender that when Major Sawyer came to ask him to wait, he would be back soon. Then he trailed Trumble into the blistering, blinding street. It was dismally deserted. No longer did the heavy ore wagons churn the grit into fine powder, no longer did the long strings of supply freighters roll in from the railroad. A pair of small boys played mumbletypeg in the old, deep-worn ruts and looked up in suspicion as the men passed. Savage, at Trumble's side, walked morosely on to the foul-smelling courthouse and along the hall to the commission office.

He nodded without speaking to the assembled men. Dale Chum he knew to speak to, and Wallace, the bank cashier beside Simpson, the bank president. Savage did not believe Simpson was on the commission and wondered why he was here. The last man at the table he could not place, a small, wiry redhead with a bridge of freckles across his nose. He was introduced as Henry Malcomb, the new county judge. The table they sat at was wide and no one extended a hand. Savage dropped his hat on it and took a chair facing them.

Simpson spoke first in a deprecating tone. "I think Trumble is wrong, Savage. I don't believe you or anybody else can get rid of this deplorable situation."

Savage said nothing. He did not like the banker's pomposity and he had the cattleman's natural distrust of moneymen. Too many ranchers had been squeezed and foreclosed on in bad years. And Simpson was gross, with small pig eyes. The Colonel gave Dale Chum a head wag of sympathy as

Trumble challenged the banker.

"I tell you John Savage can do it. I rode with him and I know how he handles things."

Savage spoke directly to Chum, ignoring Simpson. "Tombstone can be cleaned up." He felt the banker's scoffing eyes on him.

When Chum looked at him with troubled eyes and said in a hollow, trembling voice, "Please, Colonel . . ." Savage nodded shortly.

Trumble let out an audible sigh of relief, lifted the gold star from the middle of the table and pinned it on Savage's vest.

"You are hereby appointed sheriff for the interim until we can hold an election and make it permanent. How many deputies will you want? I'll have to warn you the county is very short of funds."

"One's enough. Somebody to stay in the office while I'm out, and to make tax collections. I won't be bothered with that."

"One?" Simpson's grunt was scornful. "That's a bad joke if you mean it."

Savage rounded on him, his voice chill. "I mean it. And I mean this. I am to have a free hand to go after whatever man or men I choose without any interference from you people."

They conferred hurriedly and agreed

reluctantly to the condition. Savage took off the badge and dropped it on the desk.

"I need some time to arrange to leave the ranch. A week or so, and to find a place to stay here."

He did not wait for their reaction but put on his hat and walked out, leaving a babble behind him.

CHAPTER 4

Major Sawyer was waiting when Savage returned to the Oriental. It was his custom to pay for the beef he bought in advance, before the Colonel's crew made the delivery drive. He handed over the check, they had a leisurely drink together.

Afterward Savage visited the bank to make his deposit and spend a few moments assuring Verne Hannah that his sister was well and happy at the ranch. Savage had helped arrange a position for the boy in Simpson's bank at a low salary and was increasingly concerned that he often borrowed money from Edna, money that was never repaid. Verne still lived with his parents and allowed that at last his father was keeping his head above water in the small store, largely because John Savage bought his supplies from him.

In late afternoon he rode home, arriving at the corral at dusk. His wife was there, sitting on the top rail watching a pair of frisky colts circle the enclosure. The crew was out on roundup, only Edna and Sam were left at headquarters and the ring of iron on iron indicated that the black rider was in the blacksmith shop. Savage pulled saddle and head gear off the sweated gray, turned it in with the colts and climbed to the rail beside his wife. She nudged his shoulder fondly without turning her head, still watching the young horses.

Seeing the quiet pleasure in her face, Savage told himself again how fortunate he was to have found this woman. She had brought more to the marriage than the domesticating of John Savage. Her steady intelligence matched his well and he had learned to rely heavily on it. Further, most women would have been frightened of the lonely country, of outlaws and roving Mexican smugglers. Edna had never shown fear. She loved the land, the cattle, the horses.

She had showed her strength early when Savage hired ten Mexican youngsters and took them on a cattle-buying trip to Magdalena, below the border, carrying a sack of gold for the purchase. Don Miguel, owner of the cattle, had warned Savage of a gang of bandits drinking in the little cantina of the neighboring village. Miguel would not keep the sack at his hacienda for fear the bandits would raid him.

Savage had alerted his new riders to be watchful but they had panicked and deserted. One rode back to the Lazy S and reported that Savage had been murdered. It was midnight after the second day and the regular riders were sleeping. Not waiting to wake them, Edna had taken a loaded rifle, hitched the buckboard and whipped the team south to find her husband's body before scavengers got to it. All night she drove through the empty country and at daybreak saw a dust cloud moving toward her, a cattle herd. Closer, she made out her husband's ramrod-straight figure in the lead and stopped the buckboard so it would not spook the animals. When he came up, worried that she was alone, she said she had been told he was dead.

His story was that no one in Magdalena dared help him for fear of reprisals. He had built an early campfire, left it burning and climbed up a steep, narrow canyon, leaving a conspicuous trail. Hidden in boulders near the top, he had watched until the bandits filed up, a single line because there was not room to ride abreast. They were full of tequila and careless and Savage had shot three off their horses before the others bolted down and kept going in a drunken rush out of the territory. Savage had stayed in the boulders until morning, then gone to Miguel for the herd and borrowed his vaqueros to drive them north.

Now as they sat atop the fence she turned to him, smiling. "The major make the usual contract?"

"Uh-huh. A thousand head."

"Was he late? What took you so long?"

"Talk in town."

When he was troubled Savage had an unconscious habit of massaging his leg where the Minié ball was lodged and gave him dull pain. From the corner of her eye Edna saw him rub the thigh rhythmically.

"Out with it, John. What's wrong?"

He felt oddly tongue-tied facing this need to explain himself. "Lew Trumble's commissioners made me sheriff. I got baited into taking the job. Franklin quit."

She sat silent, absorbing the shock of his words. It was totally unlike her husband to drop such a bomb out of nowhere. She was so accustomed to his ruminations, his casting back, to the sides, forward, searching for perspectives from which to make his judgments. She had had no hint of any such extraordinary move as this. She approached the subject cautiously.

"You? A southern rancher? Did you think it through or did you decide on impulse? What did they use for bait?"

"Little Betsey Chum. Several men grabbed her off the street in broad daylight and mauled her. She may lose her mind." His tone was flat, bleak.

Edna's breath gasped in. After a long moment she burst out in frustration, "That vile town."

"Not vile. Helpless. There's no one left to ride herd on it. Old banker Simpson said nobody could, said I couldn't. I can."

"You could, yes." She closed her hand over the fingers that worked his leg. "But why? You have always maintained that a man should look out for himself and his, not meddle in the affairs of others. And you've never been goaded into doing anything you haven't thought clear through. Why now?"

"I did think it through." He gave her a sheepish smile. "On the way home, after I'd said yes. Lew Trumble pointed out something I hadn't ever considered. I am a citizen of this county and Tombstone is an affair of mine now. We've taken a fine living out of Arizona and we owe something back. There comes a time when you must stand up and be counted and this is my time. There's no one else to do what must be done, as much as I dislike the choice."

She read the dull burning anger in his face, in the agate hard eyes, and bent to kiss his cheek, then spoke softly.

"All right. I understand. You had better ride out in the morning and tell the boys before they hear about it from someone else and quit in a bunch. Now go tell Sam it's time to wash up for supper."

She was particularly tender to him that night after the meal, during which Savage heard the first ominous rumble, like distant heavy thunder, in the black man's protest, the warning of a probable revolt by the crew. In the morning Edna made him his favorite breakfast, thin venison steak barely braised on a thick bed of hot salt. Afterward she walked with him to the corral, where the tight-lipped Sam had the gray saddled, and stood with Savage's oldest friend watching him ride off across the rolling land toward the roundup camp.

"I feel so sad for him today," Edna sighed.

"Uh-huh." The black man sounded bitter. "He's a good man. Too good for them townie commissioners to lay this on him. He's riding for sure trouble from now on. But I stay with him anyhow."

The noon sky stretching over his head held not a trace of cloud to fend off the fierce sun. The camp, as he approached, stank of roundup smells and was loud with the sounds of animals and men. He had timed his arrival for grub call but he was a little early and he paused near the branding fire, noting the strong grace as Bo Roberts kneeled, earmarking a calf, smearing the cut with *tecole* to keep screw worms from burrowing in, then kicked the young steer to its feet and watched it bound away, the tail crooked high at an angry angle.

Roberts rose and headed for the wash-up trough outside the temporary corral. Savage walked his horse after him, swung down, pulled the gear off its sweating back and turned it in with the others, then joined Bo where the foreman ducked his head under water to scrub neck and face and scrape at the grit in his scalp. Savage nodded when the man came up for air and scoured the trail dirt from his own face and hands. Neither spoke so Savage judged that word of his new office had not penetrated this far out.

Gasper Jones began beating his iron rod around the inside of the triangle at the cook wagon, parked a good way upwind of the center of activity. Savage walked beside Roberts to the rear of the wagon, where they filled tin plates from the stack on the tailgate, then hunkered down on their haunches out of the way. Most of the crew was straggling in, leaving the rest to hold the animals yet to be marked. Those would eat when they were relieved. Everyone was too tired for talk.

Savage took his time over the boiled beef and beans, sopping up what chili his knife would not hold with a cone of tortilla. Gasper had lived on the border so long he cooked Mexican style, which suited the crew fine. More than half of them came from below the border. Though he had been raised in west Texas, Savage did not share the average Anglo's disdain for the people of old Mexico. His hands were rated solely on their abilities and cooperation. Mario Valdez, for instance, was valued as highly as Bo Roberts and Old Sam.

When his plate was wiped dry and his cup empty Savage took them to the rinsing tub and slid them in. Later Gasper and his kid helper would scrub all utensils with sand, then rinse them in clean boiling water. As a ranch cook Gasper was meticulously clean. A long, withered, cadaverous man, he was the butt of a standing joke that he had been dead for years but was too stubborn to lie down. A riding accident had made him unfit for saddle work and Savage, not knowing how else to use him, had given him the chuck wagon and discovered an unsuspected talent. He was still at the tailgate ladling grub for riders now coming off the holding line. Other men were lingering there, pouring second cups of coffee, when Savage and Roberts dropped their dishes in the tub.

The newest man on the crew, a youngster wandered in from Texas, had energy left for a hello.

"What's new at headquarters, Colonel?"

The question was the opening Savage had been waiting for. He lifted his voice just enough to reach all those gathered at the wagon.

"Nothing new there, but there's something from town. The county commissioners asked me to stand for sheriff. I said I would."

With the noon rest under their belts the men had begun to talk. All sounds and motions stopped abruptly. The idea that any cattleman, owner or rider, would pin on a law badge was beyond belief here. Lawmen and cowmen were enemies. Savage knew this and shared the distrust to a large extent, but the circumstances of this case had forced him into the new position. It was a call to duty, the kind of call he had spent much of his adult life answering. He expected his crew to understand when they heard the reasons. He did not expect to be challenged by his own men. But he was faced with immediate hostility.

Mario Valdez put it into words. "Boss, why do you want to do a crazy stunt like that?"

Savage hesitated. He was not in the habit of giving anyone except Edna an account of his decisions, but he saw by their manner, by the stunned expressions, that it went deep, their belief that he had betrayed their trust.

Holding Mario's eyes, he said flatly, "A woman was raped in Tombstone by a number of men the other day."

The Mexican threw out his coffee dregs in exasperation. "Serves her right for being out alone at night."

"Not at night." Savage held his tone patient. "The middle of the day. A respectable lady. A bunch yanked her into an empty store as she was going shopping. It has to stop. Someone has got to get on top of that town."

Valdez bared his teeth in an angry snarl. "Let it kill its own snakes. You are a rancher, not a tinhorn law sharp like that bastard Earp."

Savage knew the background of that

particular hatred. Valdez had been with him in Dodge after a trail drive. He had got drunk and tried to shoot up the street. Earp had disarmed him in front of an audience, ordered him to leave the camp and not come back. Chagrined, Mario would have gone for a rifle and laid for the marshal if Savage had not stopped him, threatened to fire him and taken him out of Dodge before he got himself into serious trouble.

The Colonel looked at the circle of shocked faces. About two thirds of the Mexicans were boys he had taken on after settling in the San Pedro. Brought up as vaqueros, they were fine riders, experts with cattle. These had not been up the trails to tangle with marshals and never visited Tombstone, where they were looked down on. He thought he could count on them to stay with him. The other third had come up from Texas in his trains and he had always considered them personal friends. Now their expressions gave him doubts, and it was time he must put them to the test.

"Mario," he said steadily, "we always have let it kill its own snakes, but it no longer can. I am the only man left around who can make those streets safe for their women. I don't want the job but I can't refuse to help."

Valdez glared back, unyielding. He had been with Savage longer than anyone except the original Texans. His Italian grandfather had been a section hand on the Mexican railroad and his father one of the Mexican rebel leaders. Mario was fearless, a vaquero who could ride anything on two or four legs. He was married to an Opata squaw from central Chihuahua, an artist at basket weaving, working the rattlesnake-in-the-grass pattern with the skill inherited from a thousand generations. As proud as he was unafraid, he was the one who broke the horses and for that drew an extra five dollars a month. Only Bo Roberts made as much. Behind Roberts and Sam, Savage thought of Valdez as the best man he had, and his wife was Edna's trusted confidante.

The vaquero planted his feet wide and hung his thumbs in his belt, his words choking. "Colonel, in Mexico I promised myself I would never work for a lawman. They are not friends of our kind. My father was killed because a Rurale captain wanted his horse. I shot that captain. That was when I came north and joined the Lazy S. Please, boss" — it was as near a sob as anyone had ever heard from Mario — "don't put on that star. I don't want you bushwhacked for busting a head."

Savage regarded him impassively. "You want to draw your time?"

"Don't *want* to. Have to."

The Colonel looked squarely at each of them in turn. "Anybody else that stubborn?"

There was a chorus of groans. Slowly three who had come up from Texas shoved to their feet and set their coffee cups on the tailgate of the chuck wagon, indicating they were quitting. No one else moved. Savage had won the gamble on the whole but he deeply regretted losing Mario Valdez.

"Ride on in," he said evenly. "Tell Edna to pay you off. I'll be along later."

He watched them go, Mario's spine so rigid it seemed to bend backward.

"Bo," he told Roberts, "you'll take my place until this mess is finished. I'll have to be in town for a while. Keep me posted from time to time."

CHAPTER 5

When the roundup crew went back to work John Savage mounted his gray and turned homeward. He was riding away from everything he loved. Everything he understood. His loyalty to his crew had always been matched by their loyalty to him, and now he was leaving them to take on a job he loathed, a thankless job of pulling a dying town out of its death throes.

He knew it had to be done. Already a man dared not lay a tobacco sack on a bar and look away from it. It would have disappeared when he turned back. He could no longer leave a horse tied at the rail while he went into a store, but must shut it in the livery corral where the hostler could watch it.

Wyatt Earp had kept such mischief-makers out of his towns. Even Johnny Behan had seen that women were safe and doors need not be locked, for the outlaws he tolerated did not stoop to such petty crimes as were rife now.

He rode warily. With the word spread in Tombstone that John Savage was now sheriff he would have to watch his back more closely than ever. Mario was right in that some braggart was likely to think he could get rid of the new officer with a back shot. That first dusk he made camp in the open, built a small fire and sat until dark. Then he left his blanket roll and, keeping low not to make a moving bulk against the skyline, went to a rockburst to watch for anyone approaching the fire.

In time, as the flames died, someone did, a man who rode in boldly and stepped down to feel along the blanket, straightened facing the rocks for a long moment, then mounted and rode off to the arroyo the trail paralleled. The Colonel's smile was thin but warm. He had an outrider keeping track of him. Mario Valdez, who had laid back to escort him, and whose pride would be bruised if he knew he was discovered. Savage's hope rose that the vaquero had changed his mind, that he would find him at the Lazy S when he got there.

But he did not. At the corral fence he tossed his reins to Sam, who said nothing but looked downcast, then he moved on to the house, where Edna heard his boots on the breezeway and met him at the door.

"I am so sorry," she said, and took him in her arms. "The whole family left. I lent Mario the buckboard to leave in town. What about the other boys?"

"The important ones stood hitched." He was more somber than she had ever known him. "But I'd trade most any five of them for Mario. I have to live with my own conscience, why can't he understand that?"

"He just hates lawmen so much he doesn't think."

Sam joined them for supper as usual when the crew was gone. It was his self-appointed responsibility to stay close and watch over Miss Edna when they and the Colonel were away. Normally his talk was easy, ranch related, but this night he was mute and to ease the atmosphere Savage made a joke of Valdez, secretly following him to within half a day's ride of the ranch.

"If you see him again don't either of you let on," he finished.

Sam grumbled, "I just wish he would stay around, keep on doing that. Colonel, you're going to need eyes in the back of your head if you go sheriffing."

"I've got them, and extra ears too. Sam, did you ever know me to be caught out? You going to stay here with the crew or will you go to town with us?"

"I'm going wherever Miss Edna goes. She's going to need me close in that den of snakes."

The next morning John Savage spent alone, wandering among the scattered structures that made up the headquarters cluster, half of his mind calling himself a damned fool for letting anyone so disrupt his life. The Valdez house was empty and silent. No children ran and whooped in the yard. Mario had built it two years after the Colonel's log home was finished, when he had brought his Opata bride to the Lazy S on returning with a herd from Mexico.

The vaquero had not used timber, preferring to make his three-room cottage of 'dobe bricks, a mix of earth and straw, dried, laid up and plastered yearly so the rains would not wash out the walls. The roof was flat, supported by slender pine poles that extended through the upper foot of the mud walls with stub ends exposed that held clay *ollas* of cooling water and braided strings of chili peppers drying in the sun. Around the unfenced yard Rosa had planted fleshy pancake-shaped cactus for a vegetable and red geraniums to please the eye.

Rosa, barely five feet tall, had grown stout in her years here, with strong arms and legs.

All the crew had loved her. She was never too busy to sew on a button or repair a tear in a rider's jeans and her molasses cookies were a treat after Gasper Jones' dried-apple pies. But Savage knew that Edna would miss her most. The family would, he supposed, return to Mexico.

The whole headquarters area looked and sounded abandoned and foreboding. Even Sam was not in evidence, engaged with Edna sorting clothes for packing.

In the afternoon a buggy brought Lew Trumble with the news that he had a furnished house cleaned and ready for the Savages and an election had been called for the next week. Several terms of office would run out soon and, to save the county cost, new candidates would be chosen at the same time as the sheriff, to stand by until the incumbents left. The Colonel agreed to be in town by election day. The ranch was incredibly lonely this afternoon and he would have preferred to leave at once, but he meant not to be pushed another inch.

Even Edna, unusually quiet through the days since Rosa and the children had gone, was willing to leave by the time they did go. Savage had brought back the buckboard in which Mario had hauled his belongings away, loaded it again with what Edna decided they should take and left Bo Roberts a note telling him to have it picked up at the O.K. Corral after roundup was finished. When it was emptied at the town house Savage dropped it and the team at the livery and walked back along nearly empty Allen Street.

He imagined that Mario Valdez was in Mexico by now and stopped short when an apparition turned the corner; he hardly recognized the vaquero. The hair, which had been worn lank, shoulder-length and contained by a band woven by Rosa, was cut short in the fashion of townsmen, under a derby turning green with age. Hot as it was, Mario had on a black woolen suit that hung loose on his spare frame. His face, the drooping mustachio shaved off, had a sultry handsomeness Savage had not been aware of before. The rider looked through Savage until the Colonel stepped in front of him and blocked his path.

"Valdez? I hardly knew you. Thought you were long gone."

The Mexican's olive skin under his tan flushed in embarrassment, then his jaw thrust out, challenging.

"No star, Colonel? You come to your senses?"

"I won't wear it until I'm elected."

Valdez' lip turned up at one corner. "Tomorrow. Guess I can still talk to you today. I've got a job here driving the banker's carriage, being bodyguard for Simpson's wife and daughter when they shop."

"In that getup?"

Valdez' black eyes were sheepish, his voice a trifle loud, as if to convince himself. "Simpson's orders. He got too big for them and made me buy them."

John Savage concealed the shame he felt for his old horse breaker. He had never known a more independent rider than Mario Valdez, self-confident, even cocky, never taking backtalk from anyone. He must want to stay in Tombstone very badly to put up with the banker and his haughty wife. They would not be easy people to work for.

He wondered aloud, "You like this, after the ranch?"

For a split second Mario's full mouth turned down, then he brought his lips up to a fixed smile. "It's better for us in town. The kids can go to school. The pay's good, I get regular hours off and it's a lot easier taking care of the team than getting pounded on an outlaw horse. And" — of a sudden his old sparkling grin flashed and he struck a pose — "you've got to see the house Simpson's selling me. You in a hurry?

Rosa would be glad to see you."

"Let's go." Savage fell in beside the Mexican's long, smooth stride. "Edna misses her and the youngsters. You going to be stiff-necked about them seeing each other too?"

Valdez made no answer and Savage dropped the subject. With all of them in the town together he hoped that nature would take its course, that the old friendships would soon erode the barrier. In silence Mario turned up a side street to an imposing residence set flush with the wooden sidewalk, a two-story structure in a town that ran to a single floor, iced with lacy gingerbread and stained-glass windows. Above the narrow porch the ornate red glass lamp was still bracketed.

"Suzie Golff's place?"

John Savage could not keep his astonishment out of his voice. It had not been the largest whorehouse in Tombstone, but an exclusive one catering to mine owners, superintendents and the wealthier businessmen. The Colonel had never been inside and neither Mario Valdez nor any other member of his crew would have been admitted, but he had heard gossip of its elegance before the madam and her stable had decamped.

"You say Simpson is selling it to you? Did

he buy it from Golff?"

Mario took the steps at a jump and shoved the door open, his eyes sparking mischief. "He always owned it. The woman just ran it for him. Come on in and look it over, you won't believe it."

Savage found that he disliked banker Simpson more than ever, a hypocrite as well as a high-handed bully. They entered an anteroom, then a parlor separated by an arch hung with beaded curtains. The room was furnished with heavy, red velveteen upholstered armchairs, a horse-hair couch, a mahogany bar with a crystal mirror and a small pump organ. At the rear a flight of stairs to an upper hall was framed by a mahogany banister.

Valdez shouted for his wife and she came through a side door, the two round-faced, round-eyed boys and the Indian-looking little girl peering from behind her. When they saw Savage all three whooped and ran to circle him, dancing and grinning. Rosa herself flung her purple voluminous outer skirt over her head and clamped her hands around her cheeks, crying through her fingers.

Savage said in Spanish because English was still difficult for her, "You're a sight for lonesome eyes, all of you. The ranch is like boot hill without you."

"Fix some tacos and drinks, *madre*," Mario told her. "While I show off our hacienda." Leading Savage up the curving stairway, he dropped his tone. "Rosa and the kids think this was a hotel. Some hotel, Colonel."

With an exaggerated flourish he unlocked a gilded door and ushered Savage into a small but expensively decorated sitting room hung with saccharin watercolors of cherubim in gilt scroll frames, then into a bedroom where a large bed occupied the center of the floor and full-length mirrors glittered, covering walls and ceiling. There Suzie Golff had entertained her wealthiest guests and they watched themselves at play.

"The bridal suite." Mario rocked with laughter.

CHAPTER 6

In the mining camp election day had always been its own excuse for celebration. True, the saloons were closed but everyone knew that in advance and stocked up on jugs. Before noon Tombstone was full of people, not as crowded as in its heyday but the whole county had turned out and a good proportion of those on the streets were already drunk.

No one was running against Savage and he was the target of threats by the toughs that he would be run out of the territory as soon as he pinned on the star. Contests for the other offices were fierce. Paying jobs were increasingly hard to come by and by three o'clock there had been fistfights on every street and Rafter Green had shot himself in the foot.

Rafter was six feet ten inches tall and Doc Combs won himself a lot of laughter when he dug the bullet out by saying it took quite a marksman to hit anything at the distance Rafter's foot was from his hand. Green was running for city council on the Democratic ticket, as everyone else was. All the Arizona towns voted Democratic, which was the reason the Republican Earps had never gone further in local politics. Rafter had taken umbrage with his opponent, Cal Clements, for jibing that he was too illiterate to write his name, and had been drawing his gun with the announced intention of stuffing it down Clements' throat when it went off. The .45 slug dug into Rafter's instep.

John Savage sat out the day with his wife and Sam at the house. Until the votes were counted and he pinned on the gold badge he meant not to become involved with the infractions of the celebrants. When the polls had closed, the bars opened and those men who could still keep their feet repaired to them to drink and play cards and lay bets on who the winners would be.

The count took most of the night. When it was finished the commissioners posted a bulletin of the results on the courthouse door, locked up and went home to sleep. They met again in the morning, sending a messenger around to the newly elected, calling on them to appear for swearing in. John

Savage was asked to come in first.

By the time he reached the courthouse the saloons were silent and the small gathering around the door was exclusively female. Lew Trumble's wife led a welcoming delegation, pumping Savage's hand, then stretching to plant an impulsive kiss on his cheek.

"Sheriff, we're all so relieved. Lew promises that you will soon make a respectable community out of Tombstone for the first time in its history. Thank you."

Her gushing embarrassed Savage and he wanted no woman's hand on him except Edna's. He broke loose and stepped away.

"It will take some time." He was curt. "Meanwhile you ladies continue to lock up and take care. Go home now before the men start waking up to make trouble."

Belle Trumble gasped and backed off, starchy with affront. Savage did not wait for more. He circled the delegation and escaped through the door. The commissioners were waiting, sitting at the table with coffee mugs before them, looking bleary-eyed after the night's work. Simpson was one of them, though in what capacity Savage did not know.

Bobby Burch was also there, a middle-aged, thin man who had been deputy under the previous sheriff and kept the peace as best he could during the interim before the election. Savage had asked him to stay on since he knew the routine of booking the arrested, which the Colonel did not.

Dale Chum was spokesman this time, saying portentously, "Congratulations, Sheriff. Now that you are in office don't you want to change your mind and put on a couple of more men to help? Burch isn't going to do much good."

The deputy winced at the inference that he was not capable. Savage winked at him.

"He's enough to sit on the jail and collect taxes and do what he's been doing. He's to have a free hand the same as I will."

They wanted to haggle now, wanted it spelled out just what Savage considered a free hand. He cut the interview short, saying he wanted to be on the street with Burch by the time the election celebrants brought their hangovers outside. He stood impatiently while Lew Trumble again pinned on the star, beckoned Burch with him and left. When the door was closed the deputy gave him a sidewise scrutiny.

"I'll go along, you'd best stop by your office." The tone was impassive with some judgment withheld. "You've got visitors. The Tucson Ring is calling. Jack Seers and Benson Hodges."

Not being a politician, John Savage had not counted on such a visit. The Tucson Ring was a powerful group who controlled the state legislature and were generally reputed to be a gang of crooks, but the Colonel had supposed Tombstone to be in too dire condition to be worth their notice.

"How come, Bobby?"

"They'll let you know plain enough."

On the street the women were gone and no one else was about. Burch turned one way, Savage the other, toward the sheriff's office with four cells behind it. Two well-dressed, soft-handed men were there, one in Savage's swivel chair as if he belonged there, the other in one of the straight chairs against the wall. Their clothes told nothing of who or what they were, only the big diamond rings both wore indicating wealth. They had on knee-length coats of fine fabric that might spell gamblers, gray striped trousers tucked into expensive boots, and flat-crowned black hats with wide, curled brims lay on the desk. They blew smoke from the finest cigars and introduced themselves. Seers occupied the swivel chair, Hodges the other. Neither reached for Savage's workhard hand.

The Colonel knew the names although he had never met the men. But he had had brushes with their representatives and had not liked their approach. They raised no cattle, performed no legitimate service but got fat off the public till acing as brokers, middle-manning sales of beef to the Indian agencies and army posts. Several times Savage had been warned that unless he operated through the Ring his markets would be cut off. So far he had been able to hold those markets alone.

Their hirelings had threatened and had used outlaws to attack his drives when he was delivering cattle but his crew had beaten off the raids. Lew Trumble had told him the Ring tried to find someone to run against him, but no one would take the risk of touching Tombstone. He judged they were here to buy him, acting as if they already owned the place. Jack Seers did the talking, a paunchy, thick-legged man who could not pull his knees together. He had an unruly bristle of beard, a rat's nest of mismatched red hairs around a bee-stung pouting mouth that sprayed spittle when he spoke. After his first words Savage retreated out of range.

"Sheriff." He puffed like a steam engine. "You know that since the mines closed Cochise County is about the poorest corner of the United States. But we Tucson people take care of our own. You just accept a place on our steering committee and we'll see you don't lose at the next election. There'll also be something on the side to help out your cheap-John salary."

The Colonel looked from one to the other with cold distance. "Not interested."

Seers sounded astonished. "Not interested? You're in politics now, man, and no politician has any clout in the territory unless he's a member in good standing in our state organization."

John Savage's voice was quiet, even, without emphasis, but it carried a threat like a kitten with its claws retracted.

"Listen good, both of you. I don't repeat. I don't give a damn about politics. I took a one-time job to clean up this county and that's what I'll do. Anyone who gets in my way will be hurt. Keep out of Cochise County. I don't care what you do in Tucson or Prescott or the rest of Arizona, but don't get underfoot here."

Their faces had turned so red Savage expected veins to burst. Their mouths fell slack and their eyes bugged; then they dropped their eyes, stood up and clamped on their hats. Seers started to say something more, changed his mind and they marched stiffly through the door, leaving it open.

When they had gone Savage let a small, tight grin touch the corners of his lips. That evening he reported the visit to his wife.

"It beats all what crawls out from under rocks and puts on pants. The whole crowd would rather steal a dollar than make it honestly."

"The deeper you get into this mess the worse it gets. John, you can't fight the whole territory."

"Why not?"

Edna Savage sighed. All her life she had watched her father fail at one business after another, always blaming his misfortunes on organized authority and politicians, and a belief in their corrupt power was ingrained.

"Maybe you think you can," she said doubtfully. "But I wonder."

Chapter 7

In the years when he had been trailing herds John Savage had watched the cow-town marshals control the cowboys in the Kansas railroad settlements. He had seen them handle such rugged individualists as Shanghai Pierce, One-armed Reed and other of the south Texas cattle barons, and while he had been, in a sense, on the other side of the fence, he had admired the neat and efficient way in which the Wyatt Earps and other lawmen mastered their problems. Earp had been singularly direct. He carried a heavy .45 known as a Buntline Special, given him by the writer Ned Buntline. This gun had a sixteen-inch barrel, an apt weapon for buffaloing, clubbing a man over the head; many an obstreperous trail hand had waked in a cell with a headache he could not blame on rotgut whiskey. It was a popular method among other marshals.

Savage considered using it and discarded

the idea. He was not as tall as Earp, with the leverage of a clean blow downward. Further, the Buntline was too cumbersome to please him. He preferred his Peacemaker, a single-action .45, a gun made in two barrel lengths, the seven and a half favored by army officers, and a smaller five and a half. Savage carried the shorter, the barrel finely engraved ahead of a diamond-set pearl grip. It was not suited for buffaloing. It was built for one use only, to shoot with.

During his first ten days in office the Colonel had shot no one. The toughs had so far made no moves against him, watching to learn his routine and the patterns he would establish. He had not yet succeeded in making a dent in the infestation of thieves, burglars and others who tormented the town.

He had brought in man after man only to watch helplessly as Judge Henry Malcomb ordered small fines and turned them loose. After the first six had walked away free Savage protested to Malcomb. The judge pointed out that the crimes the men had been brought in for were only misdemeanors carrying limits on the amount that could be levied. In two cases the only evidence the sheriff had was hearsay and so not admissible in court. Frustrated, John Savage demanded a hearing by the commission.

Facing them, Savage said bluntly, "Malcomb has that riffraff laughing at me. Is that the way you want it, Judge?"

The judge said stiffly, "Certainly not, Sheriff. But you're new at the law. There's more to it than just arresting. If you don't bring me solid, proper evidence and I act on anything less, a higher court will reverse my decision on appeal. It would be a waste of my time and a mark against my record."

Savage looked at one face after another. "Do you want this place cleaned up or not? Yes or no."

A chorus said yes.

"Then get out of my way."

Lew Trumble said hurriedly, "What have you got in mind, John?"

"From here on any time I catch anybody doing anything I know he shouldn't I'll give him a time limit to get out of the county and stay out, and he'll understand what I mean."

"And if they refuse to leave?"

"We'll see."

Judge Malcomb used his hand against the table as if it were a gavel. "That's illegal, Sheriff. You can't take the law into your hands, be judge and jury on your own."

"I say I can. Who's going to stop me?"

"You'll be liable for arrest yourself."

"Who will arrest me? Burch? I think not."

Savage slammed his hat on and left the meeting. Lew Trumble went after him, caught him in the hall and stopped him.

"I don't blame you for being hot under the collar, Sheriff. I feel the same way. They clubbed you into this spot and now they're backing down from the only way you can get anywhere. Now here's something else to watch out for. Pistol Pete Slocum. He's the kind that brags about the notches in his gun. You arrested a friend of his last week."

"And by-the-book Malcomb turned him loose in five minutes."

"I know, and it makes them all bolder than before. I heard Slocum say he's got you sized up and you've got a ring in your nose that he's going to cinch his rope on. He has a tie-in with the Tucson crowd, which makes him doubly dangerous."

Savage's voice was dry, noncommittal. "I picked up the rumors, Lew. Just keep your head down."

Trumble turned back to the committee room and Savage left the courthouse, headed for the sheriff's office. A group of loafers squatted on their haunches against the wall of the Alhambra saloon across the street, one of them Pete Slocum, a swaggering giant with a slow-witted, knife-scarred face. As Savage passed he heard the man's raucous caw, the voice raised to carry.

"No need to be scared, boys, he ain't got no teeth. Hey, Sheriff, I like that big gray you ride around on. I'm claiming him."

Savage went on as if he had not heard, the group's laughter trailing him. He had been itching for a week to find a reason to handle Slocum but so far there had been no cause. Brassy talk was not sufficient, the man must make a first move, and the Colonel thought now that his patience would soon pay off. In the office he closed the door and stood back from the window, where the letters painted on the glass screened him, and watched. Slocum stood up, stretched, yawned, hitched his belt higher and ambled toward the livery.

"Fine," Savage said aloud. "Keep on, go through with it."

It was not long before the man appeared again, mounted on the gray, prancing it up the street, stopping in the middle of the dusty ribbon before the office to call:

"Sheriff, come on out and see how I look on my new horse."

Savage opened the door and stepped to

the walk. Slocum sat quartered to him, his left hand on the reins tightened to pull the animal's neck into a cruel arch. His right hovered inches from his belted gun, the fingers clawed, ready to draw at the first indication of a move by Savage. Arms hanging loose, the Colonel walked to the edge of the boards, ten feet separating him from the rider.

"Get out of that saddle."

"Make me."

The tone held raw mockery. Slocum had the edge, knew it and knew the sheriff knew it. The man could snap out his weapon and fire before Savage could lift his hand to his holster. He sat waiting, his eyes beady with eagerness. The sheriff did not move either arm. He took one easy step off the walk, another across the dust, kept moving slowly until he stood almost against the stirrup. Slocum was not fool enough to kill him in broad daylight in the center of town unless by accident. With his clawed fingers poised to strike, his whole attention was focused on Savage's right hand.

Without telegraphing the move, Savage shot out his left, jerked Slocum's leg free of the stirrup and flung him off the saddle. The man fell heavily, both arms outstretched, his gun bouncing out of the holster. It was heavier than the Peacemaker. Savage scooped it up and swung it in his first try at buffaloing, catching Slocum behind one ear as he rolled, knocking him out.

The horse danced aside. Still holding the gun, the sheriff leveled it toward the loafers, watched them while he took a grip of Slocum's coat collar and backed off, dragging the limp figure out of the street, across the walk and into the office. He kicked the door shut, dropped the gun on his desk, hauled Slocum down the hall, dumped him on the floor of a cell and locked it. Then he returned to the street, locking the office.

The gray was half a block away, wandering along the edge of the walk, nibbling at the grass tufts growing there. Savage whistled. The animal twitched an ear but did not lift its head. Savage whistled more shrilly and reluctantly the horse turned and came to the sheriff.

Savage swung the trailing rein up to the withers, mounted and walked the animal over to the loafers, who watched warily. Five minutes before all four had been laughing. Now they stirred, uncomfortable under Savage's cold stare.

Rigid in the saddle, the sheriff said evenly, "You in the brown shirt, what's your name?"

The man glanced both ways at the others as if for help and found only befuddlement. "Bob Ellis."

"Have you got a job here?"

Ellis swallowed, his throat suddenly dry. "Not right now, not since the mines closed."

"Three years. We don't need you around. You have until tonight to be out of Cochise County. Draw slow and toss your gun here."

Color washed out of the man's face. "But . . . but . . ."

"There are no buts. Don't let me see you after sunset. Get your gear and clear out." Savage watched him until his eyes dropped and the gun landed in the street, then spoke to the next man. "Name?"

That one flared in anger. "Hell with you. I . . ."

He did not finish the sentence. Savage was fast, spinning out the Peacemaker, shooting off the man's hat without touching the scalp.

"Answer or the next slug goes three inches lower."

"Hough." The word came quickly.

"Gun." When that lay beside the other Savage added, "The same goes for you as for Ellis. Be out of town by sundown or be ready to come shooting. Next?"

The third gave his name as Sid Hughes, obediently threw away his weapon but argued that he had no money, no horse, no way to travel.

"Walk. Pick up your iron at the office when you leave."

The last man, Ernie Sanders, had a part-time job and also argued. "You can't float me, Sheriff. I work here."

"Where? Doing what?"

"Here at the Alhambra, mucking out mornings."

Savage hesitated for the barest instant. He did not want to cause unnecessary hardship for someone who had at least a minimal employment, but an hour's labor a day left plenty of time to make trouble.

"Sorry. You have a horse?"

The man nodded, his mouth bitter.

"Then take your friend with you, you can change off riding. Don't be around after sundown. Now all of you move off."

They rose and shuffled down the walk, hangdog and silent. The sheriff dropped off the gray, gathered the guns to lock in the office. Moans from the cell indicated Pistol Pete Slocum was coming around. Savage left him where he was, took his horse to the livery, to a stall in the shade, then returned to the office to wait for his deputy.

CHAPTER 8

Bobby Burch arrived a half hour later wearing a curious expression, as though he had picked up word of Savage's order floating the loafers and his arrest of Pete Slocum, and walked back to look in the cell for verification. A dour, indecisive man, he came to the desk sounding uncertain.

"This will make trouble quick. They aren't going to like it."

Savage had read Burch's face and followed his detour from the chair. "What 'they' do you mean?"

"Jack Seers and Benson Hodges in Tucson."

"What would make a tinhorn like Slocum important to them?"

The deputy roamed the room, frowning. "He's their triggerman here. They probably put him up to that business with your horse. I heard a rumor they're offering twenty-five hundred to anybody who knocks you off."

Savage's brows arched up in feigned affront. "Is that all? Maybe they'll raise the ante after I pull some more teeth."

Burch looked at the sheriff in bafflement. The Tucson crowd was a power to be reckoned with, yet Savage moved around Tombstone freely, as if unconscious of the many threats being made against him. He lifted his voice near a shout.

"What have you got to laugh at? For twenty-five hundred every ragtail in the bushes will be out to bushwhack you. You won't last long being so high-handed."

The sound waked Pete Slocum and he shoved to his feet, rubbing his sore head with one hand, shaking the bars with the other.

"Hey out there. When do I get out of here?"

Savage swiveled his chair and called down the hall, his voice flat. "Not until after Ben South comes through, at least."

South was the circuit rider, superior judge for the southern district of Arizona. Savage put more faith in him than in Henry Malcomb.

"You can't keep me that long," Slocum raged. "He may be a month getting here. I got the right to go before a magistrate to have bail set and be released."

"Not unless I say so." Savage stood up and told Burch, "Bring him something to eat, Bobby. I don't want him starved before we hang him. I'm going home for dinner. Lock up before you go."

Slocum was still yelling when he closed the door. It gave Savage more satisfaction than anything about this job since he had taken the office. The satisfaction was in his tone when he reported on the morning to his wife and Sam while they sat at table.

"Is it wise, John, to try to hold him so long?" Edna asked anxiously. "Isn't there danger that the other toughs might break him out? You could be killed."

"You know better." Savage lifted a corner of his mouth. "I just wish they'd try it, give me a good reason to come down hard on them."

Half under his breath Sam growled, "He's a bad one, Colonel. It was me, I'd take him out and shoot him now."

"I would if I didn't have this damned star pinned on." Savage continued eating, finished the dish of tapioca pudding and got up, rapping his knuckles on the table edge. "Well, at least four of the vermin won't be around tomorrow. It's a start. Don't wait supper for me, I want to make sure those four leave before dark."

Back at the office he sent Burch for his dinner and was surprised that Pete Slocum was silent, seated on the strap-iron bunk with a secret grin on his heavy lips. The change of mood made Savage suspicious. He did not know how to account for it. He checked to see that the guns he had taken from the loungers were still in the drawer where he had locked them, not that he distrusted Bobby Burch, but something had occurred here that made Pistol Pete look like the cat that had eaten the canary.

He waited a long hour for the deputy and when he had not returned by then locked up to look for him, increasingly uneasy. The street was blistering hot under the early afternoon sun with no breeze stirring. Savage sorely missed the open San Pedro Valley and the downdraft from the mountains that always brought refreshing coolness to the Lazy S. There was no one on the sidewalks. A lone rider came off the high prairie, trotted his horse to the corral, slapped it into the pole enclosure and moved without hurry to the feed store. Minutes later he reappeared, stood for a moment as if arguing with himself, then turned down the sidewalk and through the louvers of the Alhambra.

That left the street empty except for a dust devil that twirled down the center of the road and dissipated. Comparison between this scene and the roaring business of the town only three years earlier was sorry. The present town was Savage's, though he did not want it and had no liking for it. He had been forced here and pride would make him tame it. He would make it a safe place for anyone to live no matter how spineless they were, the townsmen as weak as their women.

He moved without haste through the heat, first to the restaurant where Bobby Burch usually ate, did not find him there and began trying the saloons. He noted that in every place he entered conversation abruptly stopped, that they watched him, those at the bars following him in the mirrors, the card players laying their hands face down. There was tension in the rooms, the same tension he had experienced in the Kansas cow-town saloons when a marshal entered. He had been on the other side of the badge then, backed by his crews and the men of other drovers who had come up the trail. The air in those places had been explosive, a single misplaced word often caused a holocaust of flying bottles, furniture, fists and sometimes gunfire.

Tombstone had been no different. That was no longer true. The really dangerous men were gone. But when in two more hours he had not located his deputy he began to suspect foul play. Bobby, wearing a star, was the enemy here, and while he did not amount to a lot as a law officer he was Savage's representative and anything that might have happened to him could be considered a blow at the sheriff.

He had just run out of places to look and stood on the empty street wondering what to do next when a strong sense of danger rose in him. He could not explain it. He had experienced such instinctive warnings before. Once when he was driving out from this town with his wife near midnight he had felt it as strongly as now. He had handed Edna the reins, told her to keep the team at a fast trot, pulled his pearl-handled gun and sat with it between his knees as they pulled past a high cactus clump.

Movement had flicked at the corner of his eye and he had swung that way, lifting the revolver. Moonlight shafted off the metal as John Ringo stepped his horse away from the dark clump with a rifle across his knees. He was bringing it up when Savage's gun glinted. The outlaw had flung his animal about, driven in his spurs and gone crashing off through the dark. Edna had kept the team trotting, watching the starlit road.

"How did you know?"

"I didn't. I just felt something was about to happen."

He had felt the same many times and trusted the warnings. He felt it now, the sense of impending, unseen threat. His eyes swiftly surveyed the hot street, found it still empty, nothing moving, not a single loafer in sight. The word had spread fast that he was rousting those who had no visible means of support.

He lifted the gun from his holster, carried it loosely as he continued along Tough Nut, his eyes raking doorways and the roof lines above, where a marksman would most likely lie in ambush, but saw nothing. Then a carriage turned in from a corner, the banker Simpson's rig, empty except for the driver, Mario Valdez.

Mario had looked through Savage without speaking since election day. Now he startled the sheriff by reining the team in where Savage stood and beckoning him over. Savage walked to the front wheel and looked up and the vaquero leaned to speak in a lowered voice.

"Did you send Bobby Burch to Benson this afternoon?"

Savage said in some relief, "No. Did he go over there?"

Mario's dark eyes were angry. "Simpson

gave me some wires to send. When I walked in the telegraph office Burch was there getting one off to Tucson. He acted like I'd caught him running an iron on another man's cow."

Savage's first reaction was that here lay the basis of his warning. "Any idea who he was wiring?"

Valdez' lips pulled back and he brought a yellow paper from his pocket, passing it down. "I got a copy from the agent."

The message was addressed to Benson Hodges, the Tucson Ring man who had visited Savage to bribe him. The Colonel read, "Savage slammed me in jail and won't take me before Malcomb. Get me a lawyer quick." It was signed Slocum.

The sheriff crumpled the paper in his left hand, shoving it into a pocket, his right still dangling his gun.

"Does Burch know you took this?"

"Not unless he doubled back. He went out right after I came in. Colonel, throw that damn badge in the commission's face and go home. You can't do any good here. Arrest one man and the Ring will just send another and another until one of them blows off your head."

Savage's jaw set stubbornly. He bent to rub at his thigh, which had begun to throb.

A rifle cracked at the same instant, the slug thudding into the wall at the rear of the sidewalk, and echoes rattled along the buildings. The bullet would have taken Savage in the throat or face if he had been upright. He crouched lower behind the wheel, his eyes raking the roofs across the street. Mario dived headlong off the high seat to his side, drawing as he dropped. On the roof opposite, a figure jacked to its knees behind the low parapet, a rifle against its shoulder, and a second shot splintered the floor boards of the carriage, showering grit against Savage's face. He moved a step, between the wheel and the rump of the near horse, back-handing his eyes, raised his gun deliberately and fired.

The lead drove the bushwhacker back. Muscular reaction straightened him to his feet, flung his arms wide, sent the rifle clattering to the roof. He stood poised so for a moment, then collapsed across the parapet, hung there, his body jerking, then, spread like a tarantula, he toppled over to the wooden awning above the sidewalk, slid down the slope and fell heavily to the dusty street.

"See?" Mario's word hissed.

Savage straightened erect, his finger still curled around the trigger, scanned the roofs again but saw no one else there, and lowered his attention to the doors across from him. Tough Nut was no longer empty. Men were boiling out of the buildings, running to stare down at the splayed man who did not move.

The sheriff caught the rein of the near horse as it reared in fright, hauled it down and held it until Valdez had leaped to the seat to fight the lines, then he stepped in front of the animals, stroked the flared nostrils unhurriedly, and when the team began to quiet crossed the dust, shouldering through the small crowd around the body.

It lay on its face. Savage used a boot toe ungently to roll it over. Bob Ellis, whom he had ordered out of town that morning, would travel no farther than boot hill. No one spoke. The faces around him gradually lifted from the dead man to the sheriff, shocked and astonished. They showed no surprise that a man had been killed. It was as if they had waited expectantly. What struck them dumb was that Ellis lay with a bullet through his stomach and the new sheriff stood over him. Without expression Savage gestured his gun toward the four largest men at the front of the circle.

"Pick him up and cart him to Clyde Hunt. The rest of you get back indoors."

He watched the body lifted by arms and legs and carried toward the undertaker's room at the rear of Hunt's hardware store. The audience drifted dazedly into the saloons. Mario Valdez sat on the carriage, the reins gathered between the fingers of his left hand, the gun in his right resting on his knee until Savage stood alone, then, swearing a silent oath, he shook the lines and drove off.

John Savage stood ramrod straight, unmoving under the awning, the pearl-handled gun in his hand hanging along his leg, all but forgotten. His mind was intent on what this attack meant. Had Ellis acted alone or in concert with the other three he had ordered out of town? Of one thing he was sure. The tension he had felt in his tour of the saloons had not been caused by the mere appearance of a law officer as he had thought. There had been a general awareness that an ambush was being laid. If Bobby Burch had been where he should have been, watching and listening, he would have had other warning than his instinct.

Savage lingered longer where he was, wondering if Bob Ellis' three cronies were not lying on other roofs waiting for him to pass. He had seen none of them since morning and the only way to learn where they were was to find them.

He began backtracking the street, keeping close to the wall in the shadow of the awning, watchful of the roofs when he had to cross the open road. In each saloon he asked the bartender if he had seen Charley Hough, Sid Hughes or Ernie Sanders that afternoon. None of them said they had until he entered the Alhambra.

Joel Morrison was behind the bar, a heavy-shouldered, paunchy man with handlebar mustaches and a bald head fringed like a monk's with carrot-colored wisps. He was not a friend of Savage's but was one of the few townsmen the Colonel held some respect for.

He stopped at the front of the bar, away from the small knot of drinkers around the far end, and asked his question in a tone too low to be overheard. Morrison did not speak but winked, tipping his head toward the door of the back room. Savage bought a drink, his throat parched after the action with Ellis, sipping it while he assessed the tension of the customers, finding them as wary as everyone had been all afternoon.

Morrison scrubbed at the bar with a damp cloth, leaning half across it, murmuring, "Watch yourself, Sheriff. Something's up."

By way of thanks Savage slapped the

counter lightly twice with his palm. He did not know what awaited him behind the closed door of the rear room, whether a volley of sudden shots, a thrown knife or some other attack. But John Savage had never turned aside from trouble and it was too late in his life to change his way. He walked along the bar, sensing the tightening of shoulders among the drinkers as he passed them. At the door he unholstered his pearl-handled gun, leveling it as he reached for the knob. The door was locked on the inside.

He retreated three steps, ran, jumped knee-high, slamming his boots against the panel and followed it through as the bolt tore loose and the wood shattered. His gun swept over the three men around the table.

"Reach."

They had rearmed themselves. A shotgun leaned against the table at Charley Hough's elbow. A rifle lay across Ernie Sanders' knees and another lay on the felt cover in front of Sid Hughes. In their instant of shock at Savage's explosive entrance their chairs shoved back, the legs screeching against the floor. Hough's caught in a crack and tipped over, carrying the man with it. The others kept their seats but froze in them. None of them went for a weapon.

"Hands."

Savage barked it sharply and all snapped their arms above their heads. He strode forward and threw the three guns one at a time through the open window into the alley without taking his eyes off the men.

"Ellis missed his crack at me," he said flatly. "Any of you want to try?"

His only answer was the quick paling of their faces.

"It's near enough sundown to move you out. Get up and march through that door, lock step."

He stood away from the opening and they moved with exaggerated care, eyes rolling toward him as they passed him. Savage had expected the men from the saloon proper to come crowding against the door but none was there. When he followed the three out he saw why. Joel Morrison held a shotgun leveled over the bar and all attention was on him. Savage trailed his prisoners with their hands folded on their heads on to the street and ordered them to the livery. In the hot late afternoon they were the only ones abroad.

He turned them in at the runway, whistled for the hostler, told him to bring rope and what to do with it, and covered them while their wrists were tied at their backs and a long lead line looped through their arms.

Then the barn man brought the gray horse. Savage mounted and towed the three back to the street. Behind him Charley Hough and Ernie Sanders yelled a protest.

"Don't we get to take our horses even?"

"No."

It was nineteen miles to Benson and full dark when they walked to the railroad station five hours later. They dropped exhausted on the platform, groaning at their blistered feet and bone-dry mouths. Savage left them lying where they were and went to call through the station agent's window.

"Give me three tickets to Tucson and charge them to the county commissioners."

"I'd have to have a paper from them to do that," the man protested.

Savage leveled his gun above the sill. The agent changed his mind. With the tickets in his pocket the sheriff walked to the trough where the gray was drinking, pumped a pail of water and with the dipper fed each man a drink. The rest of the water he poured over their heads. The train wheezed in within twenty minutes. Between himself and the conductor Savage loaded the men into the baggage car. The sheriff ordered the door locked and the prisoners not let out short of Tucson.

His parting words to them were, "Clear

out of Arizona as soon as you can and don't come back. Ever. You won't live long if you show up in the territory again."

Their expressions in the lantern light told him they believed him.

It was late when Savage returned to Tombstone, the town dark, even the saloons closed. He dropped his reins over the rail before the office, unlocked, went in and lit a lamp, carried it to the cells. He more than half suspected that as Edna had suggested Pistol Pete Slocum would have been taken out while he was gone. But the gunman was behind the bars snoring and Bobby Burch was asleep in the bunk he used at night when there were prisoners. The sheriff left quietly, not waking either. He rode the four blocks to the house, stabled the gray in the barn behind it and went upstairs to undress in the dark.

Edna Savage spoke from the bed, sounding as if she had not yet slept. "I'm relieved that you're back in one piece, John. When you didn't come until so late Sam went looking for you. Joel Morrison told him about Ellis and the riffraff you took away. You've had a hard day."

He filled and emptied his lungs, crawled in beside her, took her in his arms and laughed.

"A good day all around. We're rid of some scum and Mario went out of his way to do me a turn. First time he ever gave a sheriff any help. Damn it, Edna, I miss that boy. I miss the ranch."

She massaged his taut shoulders and kissed him. "So do I. When do you think we can go back?"

"As soon as this cleanup is finished. Not long I hope."

CHAPTER 9

John Savage slept an hour late, ate hurriedly and took the gray to the livery to be handy should he need it quickly. Bobby Burch had the office open and his and Slocum's dirty dishes stacked on the desk when Savage put his head through the door and beckoned the deputy outside where the prisoner would not overhear what was said.

On the sidewalk he took the crumpled telegram from his pocket, smoothed the worst of the wrinkles and put it in Burch's hand, watching as he read and recognized the words.

"How much do you get from the Tucson crowd?"

Burch's mouth turned down in distaste. "Damned little." He flicked the yellow paper. "Nothing for this unless you count the twenty bucks Slocum gave me. But the bastard does have a right to a lawyer."

"Not until I say so. You went behind my back."

"All right, I did. You want my badge?"

"Maybe I should but I need you for my eyes and ears. You belong to this town and I don't. People talk in front of you as if you aren't even there. You're all I have to depend on and now I don't know how far I can do that. But at least you didn't turn Pete loose. You take the street this morning, see what the talk is about yesterday."

Sulking, the deputy went for the dishes and took them toward the restaurant. Savage stepped inside, leaving the door open for whatever coolness the early day would circulate through the room. He sat at the desk looking out, seeing yet not seeing the empty dust strip. He was learning a truth he guessed the other frontier marshals had learned ahead of him. This job must be the loneliest in the world. There was no one except his wife to talk over problems with. Even Old Sam, the friend from his childhood, withdrew into himself when he mentioned anything to do with the office Sam so resented. And now his deputy was not to be trusted.

At noon he locked up and went home, wanting Edna's opinion of his decision to retain Bobby Burch and was relieved when he had explained his reasons that she agreed.

"I wish one of the boys from the ranch would take the place," she said wistfully. "If only Mario would come around he'd be the best man you could ask for."

"Even if he would I couldn't use him." Savage spoke angrily. "A border town like this wouldn't stand still for a Mexican with a badge. They'd fire me if I tried it."

She laughed abruptly. "That would suit me fine. They dragged you into this mess but I don't see anybody giving you any help. They seem more to resent your strength than appreciate it."

The words echoed back to Savage later in the day. When he went back to the office there was a note from Burch on the desk. The county commissioners were summoning him to a meeting at two o'clock in the courthouse. At a quarter to the hour Bobby Burch arrived to take his place and the sheriff left without hurry. There was a different air about the street today, a sense of furtive fear in the men who passed him, as if each thought he might be the next to be run out of Tombstone. None acknowledged him with as much as a direct look.

The commissioners were already gathered and there, too, was an uneasy chill that Savage did not understand. Most of the men avoided his eyes and the banker Horace Simpson took immediate control, red-faced and jowls quivering.

"You were warned the last time we met, sir, that you had no authority to drive men out of this town who had committed no crime. And you most certainly cannot go about murdering our citizens at your pleasure. Bob Ellis . . ."

"Fired two shots at me from that roof. I fired back." Savage spoke in a quiet tone, stunned by the accusation and slow to seek a meaning for it.

Simpson's voice rose in pitch. "I'd say he shot in self-defense after you had ridden over him roughshod. Ellis had no job, true, but his brother supported him, a brother who is influential in the capital and has demanded your recall. Now I am not a member of this board but I suggest to the commission that they require you to turn in that badge and leave us in peace."

Savage waited out the sputtering attack, seeing the hand of the Tucson Ring at work again. He turned his attention to the other men at the table, first to Dale Chum, keeping his tone even.

"Where do you stand on this, Chum?"

The father of the brutalized girl held

Savage's eyes, his own agonized, and said weakly, "This is the first I've heard of the idea, Sheriff. I'd have to think. . . ."

One after another they shrugged as if beaten until Savage looked at Lew Trumble. The one-time rider's lips twisted scornfully as he flapped a hand down on the table.

"They're all in hock to the bank, Colonel. They don't have the guts to fight him. Which is why I came to you to begin with. I say you're the only hope we have."

Simpson raged again. "I cannot condone legalized murder in this town, Savage. You will have to leave."

John Savage waited while silence drew out, then spoke a single explosive word:

"No."

They jerked against the backs of the chairs. Don Wallace, the bank cashier, craned his neck as if his collar was too tight, and his voice came hollow.

"But . . . you don't really want the job, you said. Why try to hold it?"

Savage pinned him against the chair with cold, hard eyes. "Because I finish what I set out to do. I have just begun. Today the element that has been raising hell here is thrown off stride. Pete Slocum is locked up and he'll stay there until a proper trial can be held by a judge with more gumption than

Malcomb. Four troublemakers are gone and there'll be more to follow them. I mean to run every one out of the county until none are left to break into your homes and molest your women. When that is done I will retire. Until then I will not no matter what pressure is used."

He put on his hat, settled it to comfort and stalked out, leaving even Simpson silent. The rest of the afternoon he spent in the office. No one came in with anything more to say. After supper he walked a patrol, alert for another ambush but there was none. The uncertain restlessness in the saloons was a satisfaction, giving him the hope that there would be voluntary departures by others who found they were not so tough as they had thought.

The next day was quiet as rumors of the sheriffs defiance filtered through the streets. Two more loafers slipped through the alleys to the livery, saddled, tied their bedrolls on and rode out through the hills.

The Tucson attorney George Lightner arrived at Benson on the afternoon train, rented a rig and made the nineteen-mile trip to Tombstone, reaching the livery at four o'clock. He bustled into the sheriff's office while John Savage stood looking out of the window and sank into the swivel chair as if he owned the place. Turning to him, Savage saw a small, intense man with a precisely tended mustache and black hair plastered in a flat wave against his skull. His small, black, round eyes probed into Savage's trying to stare him down. Savage disliked him immediately. He stood stiffly, silent, forcing the visitor to speak first. Abruptly the man leaned forward and placed an engraved card squarely in the center of the desk.

Savage read it without touching it, then looked back to the lawyer.

"I understand that you are holding a client of mine, unlawfully refusing to take him before the judge here." There was a biting edge to the crisp voice.

Savage said tonelessly, "I am waiting for the circuit rider."

"May I ask by whose authority you are delaying?"

Savage did not answer directly. He drew the pearl-handled gun from the holster and laid it on the near corner of the desk. The licorice shiny eyes opened rounder, then narrowed and he pointed a thin, white finger at the sheriff.

"Do not imagine you can intimidate me. I warn you of this. I will bring charges against you to the governor. You may have been elected by vote but it is in his power to remove you like this." He snapped his thumb and third finger.

Savage smiled thinly. If the governor did remove him he would be free to go home to the Lazy S and re-establish his life the way he preferred it, free of crooked politicians and spineless councilmen. The prospect gave him pleasure, but it would betoken a failure here. His first. And that prospect held less appeal. Bobby Burch came in, saw the confrontation and leaned against the wall to listen. With the deputy there as witness Lightner made a steeple of his hands under his sharp chin. He thought he had the sheriff cowed with his threat and turned waspish.

"Why have you not taken Slocum before Judge Malcomb as you should have?"

"Because he has turned loose everybody I've brought in."

"But it can be weeks before Ben South makes it down this way. You can't hold a man that long without bail."

Savage's brows arched in unconcern. "Slocum's eating free."

Lightner glared at him a moment longer, then stood up. "We'll see about this high-handedness." He walked past Savage and through the door.

Bobby Burch shoved away from the wall. "That's a bad boy to tangle with, Sheriff. He's said to be the sharpest lawyer in the territory."

"I wouldn't know about that. Bobby, chase after him and see what he does next."

What Lightner did was prance to the courthouse, to the rooms of Hal Hawser, attorney for Cochise County. Hawser was a wary political animal, one whom John Savage in his several years in the San Pedro Valley had not yet pegged because he had never given much attention to the lawyer. He had not held the county position when Savage first met him and employed him to search and assure the Colonel that he would have full water rights to the property he was staking out. After that he had ignored the man except for restrained civil greetings when they passed on the streets. He was on the commission, had sat in on the afternoon meeting, but he had made no comment one way or the other about Simpson's ranting against unwarranted roustings and accusation of murder.

Hawser came out of the courthouse with a jaunty stride, alone, and Bobby Burch beat him to the sheriff by half a block.

"More company on the way," the deputy said laconically and dropped into the straight chair in the corner where the office arsenal of long guns was racked with a chain strung through the trigger guards.

Minutes later Hawser's big frame came through the open door, his professional smile wide, showing most of his overlarge crooked teeth. He lowered a buttock on the desk corner and chuckled.

"You're raising some hell, aren't you, Sheriff? You set the commissioners on their ears yesterday and now you've got steam sizzling out of George Lightner's. I liked what you told the meeting, but . . ." He moved his thick head rhythmically from side to side, continuing to smile. His heavy voice filled the room. "The books are very clear. You cannot hold anyone for more than twenty-four hours without a hearing or asking for an indictment before a grand jury. Either way he is entitled to bail."

Pistol Pete's yell came from the cell. "I been telling him that but he won't . . ."

"Shut up, Pete." Hawser cut him short.

Savage sounded mild. "I am holding him."

"Oh, come now." The county attorney was conciliatory. "Let's not make ourselves a major problem. As it stands already when this case goes to a jury we'll be laughed out of court."

The sheriff squinted thoughtfully and kept

120

his even tone. "Which side are you on, Hawser?"

The man feigned surprise, starting. "Why, on the law's of course. My duty is to prosecute criminals, but how serious is this tempest in a teapot? Slocum was patently drunk, pretending to take your horse."

Savage's lids dropped sleepily. Unhurried, he opened the top desk drawer, lifted the ring of keys to the cell locks, tossed them once in his palm, dropped them in a pocket and walked out. Behind him Hawser sputtered, his politician's composure finally failing him. The blubbering sound pleased the Colonel. It was after five o'clock and he rode the gray to the house, relishing telling Edna and Sam the details of the day over their supper.

The black man talked to himself under his breath, then grumbled aloud. "They all ganging up on you, Colonel. Time's come to turn your back on this trash and go home where we belong."

Edna backed him up urgently. "John, I said before that you can't buck all the corruption in the territory. To be stubborn against reasonable odds is fine but to be plain mulish here is childish. Sam is right."

This evening their words only spoiled Savage's sense of satisfaction. He left the

table without his dessert and returned to
relieve his deputy.

Chapter 10

The sheriff had not expected the circuit rider for at least another week, but three days later Judge Ben South came into the office trailed by a smirking George Lightner. The suspicion rose in Savage that he had been sent for by either Lightner or Hawser or both. Whatever had brought him, Savage was glad to have him here. He was very tired of Pete Slocum's complaints and was anxious to take his prisoner before a tribune he believed would do better than slap the man's wrist.

South was a portly, pink man who came through the door carrying his hat and dabbing at his wet forehead with a handkerchief crumpled in a plump, soft hand. The pale blue eyes had an icy glint that belied the rest of him.

"Hot," he said, then immediately, "What's this I'm told about you holding an accused illegally, Sheriff?"

"I've held him for you, Judge."

"I understand. I realize that you are new to the system of justice and I'll allow for that, but this won't do. You will have to release him now."

Savage was quiet. "He stays where he is until trial time. Can you hold it today?"

He spoke confidently. Short of trying to manhandle him there was nothing they could do and the frustrated faces told him they recognized that. Certain that a trial could not be organized on such short notice, Savage had left an opening for the judge to set a date, not wanting to crowd him too far.

South's pink mouth pursed in what might be amusement. "You really are unfamiliar with procedure, Sheriff. Today is impossible but I can hold court at ten tomorrow morning. Will you notify the county attorney or shall I?"

"Maybe you had better if there's some formal wording." Now that he had won his point Savage used the excuse of ignorance to smooth the ruffled feathers.

Ben South left less hostile than he had entered. John Savage took the cell keys with him again, turned the office over to Bobby Burch and spent the rest of the afternoon riding the high prairie. He wanted to avoid George Lightner and Hal Hawser until the next morning when they must meet in the courtroom. He also wanted a taste of open air and some time to study the perspectives. If South was any kind of competent judge, if he sentenced Slocum to an impressive term for attempted horse theft, the rest of the Tombstone cleanup would be made much easier. There would be a precedent for successfully clamping down on those who were terrorizing the county.

At quarter to ten the next day Sheriff John Savage and his deputy, Bobby Burch, walked Pistol Pete, in handcuffs, between them to the courthouse. Savage thought there would have been an audience of the idle curious along the way but the three were alone on an empty sidewalk. There was a difference when they entered the second-floor courtroom. The rows of benches were jammed. A continuous murmur of voices almost drowned the buzzing of darting horse flies. Beyond the wooden railing the court clerk already sat at his desk. Ben South stood at a window, hands folded behind his back, listening as George Lightner talked rapidly in a low voice. As Savage left Burch just inside the door and prodded the prisoner forward, Lightner laughed and the judge chuckled at whatever had been said.

Pistol Pete rolled down the center aisle like a sailor just off a ship, his chest pouted out importantly, grinning, calling to men on the benches, waving his manacled arms. Savage's swift survey showed him an all-male crowd of the element he had been hired to control. None of the county commissioners were there except Hal Hawser, who sat at the prosecutor's table with a single empty chair beside him. He rose as Savage took Slocum through the railing gate, pointed at the defense table, where Slocum was to sit with his lawyer, and stepped across to speak to Savage.

"Take the cuffs off him in court, man, then come over with me."

By the time the sheriff had them unlocked Lightner was at his side with a derisive sniff and South had reached his seat behind the bench, rapping a gavel for quiet.

The clerk rose, faced the room and intoned into the partial hush, "Hear ye, hear ye, hear ye, the superior court for the southern district of Arizona Territory is now in session, the Honorable Judge Ben South presiding."

The county attorney got to his feet to the accompaniment of an expectant rustle as men behind him shifted positions. The judge settled himself comfortably and nodded across the bench.

"Mr. Hawser, do you want a jury summoned to try this case?"

"Not I, sir. It is a very simple matter of a practical joke that was mistaken. We will be content to try it before you."

South turned to the other table. "Is the defense ready?"

Lightner rose, half smiling. "We are, Your Honor, and we accede to the prosecutor. A jury is not called for."

That suited John Savage. He would rather rely on the experience of one man who had risen through the ranks of lawyers and lower judges to the circuit court presumably by ability, as he himself had risen by natural leadership over men he had begun with as equals on that first experimental drive out of the wreck of Texas. He had never witnessed a trial before, partly because of his earlier nomadic days and partly because of his lifelong distaste for involvement with the affairs of others, particularly those who huddled in towns. And because of that same distaste he would have been distrustful of any jury that might be empaneled from Tombstone's present citizens. What did disturb him was the prosecuting attorney's

127

easy dismissal of the charge against Pete Slocum as a mere prank. He might have understood the defense lawyer making such a claim, but in this frightened town Hawser's words sounded, at their least, like political suicide. Across these thoughts South was speaking.

"Mr. Prosecutor, will you call your first witness."

Hawser spoke distinctly. "Will Sheriff John Savage please take the stand." He indicated the chair at the corner of the judge's desk, followed Savage and stood facing him, one profile toward South, the other toward the benches, waited while Savage was sworn in by the clerk, then added, almost mockingly, "Sheriff, will you please describe in your own words the events that led to your arrest of the accused on the morning of June the fifth?"

Savage sat rigid, his face expressionless, turned squarely to Judge Ben South, his eyes hard and steady. He spoke in a low, deliberate voice of Pistol Pete Slocum astride the gray horse, curbing and raking it with spurs at the same time to make it dance before the office window, calling him out with the words, "Sheriff, come see how I look on my new horse." He told how the man had gloated, daring him to draw, his hand an inch above his own gun, how Slocum could have pulled the weapon and fired before Savage could touch his holster. At that distance, less than two feet, he said Slocum could not have missed killing him. He told how he had surprised the man, unseated him, knocked him out and dragged him into the jail. His voice was dispassionate, without emphasis, letting the words bear the weight of the testimony.

After his first sentence the judge had closed his eyes and sunk against the high back of his chair. Savage assumed that he was picturing the scene in his mind. When he finished, Hawser declared he had no other witnesses. The sheriff bent forward to stand up but the attorney waved him down. Lightner was advancing to take Hawser's place and stood a moment in silence, exaggerated astonishment on his face as he looked over the rows of men, at South, who had straightened and opened his eyes, and finally at Savage.

"Sheriff," he said at last, "are we to believe that you are so uncivilized as not to recognize a playful joke? Mr. Slocum is not so stupid as to steal anyone's horse in the center of town, in broad daylight and with an audience. And if he had meant to kill you he certainly would not have done so under the same circumstances. I have two witnesses here to say the whole matter was done on a dare, on a bet of a hundred dollars that Pete would not tease a man who wore a star."

There was caustic wonder in his tone. He turned briskly to the bench with a short laugh. "Judge South, I have finished with this witness and now wish to call Seth Hamilton, an employed bartender, and Walter Flower, who owns the saddlery."

South pinched his lips to stop his smile. "You may step down, Sheriff."

John Savage was appalled. He could not possibly have been mistaken. Slocum had been neither drunk nor making fun. He could still picture the hard glitter, the shallow breathing of a man poised for gunplay. He was being made to appear a fool. The loud sniggers among the audience proved how well the lawyers were succeeding in ridiculing him. South did not even gavel them down. He knew Hamilton and Flower and neither had given trouble, but they were apparently open to bribes and he had only his own word for defense. He returned to the chair beside Hawser and stared stonily at the men as they took the stand in turns, but they kept their eyes on the floor until they had told their lies and gone. Savage fought to keep his jaw muscles from working. One thing he would not do was betray the seething fury inside him. He wanted to be out of this room but he would not be driven. He listened with cold abstraction as Judge Ben South used his gavel and addressed the prisoner.

"Mr. Slocum, I find your performance in taking the sheriff's horse for any reason ill advised but I cannot believe you were motivated by a criminal intent. Therefore I fine you twenty-five dollars." He gaveled again. "This court is adjourned."

To Savage such a fine was more an insult than if the circuit rider had dismissed the case out of hand. He rose and walked, rigid and unseeing, out of the room where justice was so mocked, leaving a wave of laughter behind him. On his way down the stairs he fingered the badge on his vest, opened the pin to remove it, then roughly snapped it again. How he could exert any control over the town now he could not see. But he was not going to let it defeat him, lawyers, judges, commissioners, bankers or no.

Outside he crossed and positioned himself opposite the courthouse door, filling his lungs and emptying them in slow, even rhythm, disciplining himself back to calm. When Pete Slocum appeared, encircled by

131

applauding friends, Savage's hands had quit shaking and his voice was under command. The outlaw could not let well enough alone. He pushed out of the group and swaggered across the dust strip, grinning arrogantly.

"Nice show back there, Sheriff. Worth the price."

Savage's words came low, even, spaced. "If you are not out of Cochise County by tomorrow morning I will shoot you dead."

Slocum's mouth fell open. "You can't. . . . I've been tried and fined and that's the end of it. You can't order me anywhere."

"Why can't I?"

"Why . . ." Slocum shrugged his shoulders high and dropped them. "They won't let you."

"Who are *they*?"

"The judges. My lawyer. The county attorney."

"Which one would you say will use a gun to stop me?" Savage turned on a heel. "Tomorrow morning."

He walked away. It was a foolhardy chance, turning his back on the man he had challenged, but Savage counted on Slocum's arrogant pride to keep him from a cowardly shot while so many others looked on.

CHAPTER 11

John Savage spent the afternoon keeping track of Pistol Pete Slocum, following him from saloon to saloon, never speaking to him, standing at the bars to watch the outlaw in the mirrors, putting that silent pressure on him. Slocum paid no attention at first but the sheriff's presence put a damper on the pleasure he wanted to take in bragging about the trial. Savage's threat worried him enough that he did not dare risk crowding him by laughing at him. Soon the constraint drove him out of the place to another. Savage walked in before he was served the whiskey he had ordered and stood at the end of the bar, his eyes hard and steady, never shifting from Slocum's face. Slocum began to sweat and change bars more often, until toward five o'clock he stamped to the livery, saddled his horse and rode out of town. He took no gear, so he would be back.

Satisfied that the man was becoming un-nerved, the sheriff picked up his gray and rode home, stabled it in the barn behind the house and went in by the kitchen door. Edna, putting a dried-apple pie into the oven, smiled up at him, then saw that he was kneading his wounded leg, straightened, closed the stove and took his shoulders.

"You look worn out, John, was it a long trial? Did it go well for you?"

"It did not." Savage kissed her absently and sank into a chair at the table, stretching his tired feet before him.

Edna shrewdly poured brandy for each of them and stood before him in concern. "You don't mean Judge South let him go?"

He turned his face up, a bitter twist to his lips. "Worse even. Fined him twenty-five dollars. That in effect says that a threat against my life weighs no more on the scale of justice than somebody being drunk on the street."

Edna sipped at the brandy, then said stringently, "A very odd balance. But I am not surprised, in this place. John, you have done all you possibly could for these un-grateful, despicable people. Let us go home."

Savage was silent so long she had a lift of hope that he had finally had enough of

Tombstone and Cochise County's politics. Then he straightened his back and squared his tired shoulders.

"Not while I am being laughed at by every hooligan in town. How long until supper?"

"Half an hour. Go take off your boots and lie down. I'll call you." Her voice was low, even, accepting his decision, knowing that nothing more she could say would change his course.

He was dozing when she came to the bedroom door. Sock-footed, he padded back to the kitchen, blinking himself awake. Edna had a pan of warm water in the sink below the pump for his wash and Old Sam was moving dishes from the warmer over the stove to the dining-room table, casting sidelong glances at Savage but saying nothing audible. They ate without speaking, each husbanding his own thoughts. Edna had just brought the pie and coffee when her younger brother, Verne Hannah, came and she went for a plate and cup for him.

The man was slight of build, his face almost feminine in its softness, with none of the firm strength of his sister's. He resembled his weak father more than the others of the family. He took a chair, shaking his head, his eyes downcast.

"Damned shame what they did today,

John. I wonder that you put up with it."

Savage made no comment. He had long since given up hope for the boy's development. Verne had at least held on to his position at the bank but he was a compulsive gambler and apparently a compulsive loser. The sheriff did not know how much money his wife had poured into her brother's pockets but he guessed it was considerable.

She was deeply fond and protective of the boy who was so much younger than she, had been more mother than sister to him, and John never questioned her treatment of him. She had her own bank account into which he deposited a hundred dollars a month. Out of that she paid the household expenses and bought her clothes. Whatever was left she was free to use as she chose. It never showed up in jewelry or feminine frills and Savage judged that Verne got most of it. It irritated him that a woman as realistic as Edna was about her father's shortcomings and the faults and virtues of others seemed to have a blind spot concerning Verne. He had protested once some years before and they had come as near a quarrel as they ever had. From then on he had kept off the subject.

When the meal was finished and they stood, Verne and Sam carried the debris to the kitchen. At least when he came the boy helped with the dishes while he visited with his sister, a chore Savage normally chose for himself as an opportunity to talk with his wife in privacy when Sam had left them. Here in town it was about the only time they had alone together. But he did not interfere when Verne called.

Still without his boots, the sheriff retired to the dark porch to smoke a twisted, strong Mexican cigar, knowing that Edna disliked the odor that clung in the curtains. When it was smoldering to his satisfaction he sat in the rocker beside the front window appreciating the cooler evening air. They were four blocks from the center of the shrunken town and little noise carried this far from the saloons. The neighboring houses were dark, empty, deserted. Savage rocked idly until the small cheroot had burned to ash, knowing the people in the kitchen would be discussing the court case and his stubborn refusal to be run out, wondering what reason Verne was giving this time for needing cash. Since Savage had become sheriff the deputy had delegated himself to keep account of the poker games Verne sat in on and the approximate amount of his losses and to report on both. Savage resented that as prying, but he had said nothing about it because he needed Bobby Burch's gossip to tell him what was going on.

A slight sound snapped his attention to the street, a boot grating on stone here beyond the end of the sidewalks. Savage threw himself out of the chair forward, flat on the porch, at the same moment a high-powered rifle cracked and lead drove into the wall at the height his chest had just been. A second shot broke the glass in the front window. It splintered inward, tinkling on the floor. He heard running feet inside and his wife crying his name, his brother-in-law's shout, and yelled to both to stay back. A third bullet slammed into the post of the porch railing close to his head.

Then from the corner of the house the .50-caliber Sharps, the old buffalo gun that was Sam's favorite weapon, blasted a hole in the night and he knew the black man was at the end of the porch watching the darkness with what Savage thought of as cat eyes. If anyone could see at night like a mountain lion it was Sam.

Savage stayed where he was, spread-eagled, afraid that the moment of reaching for his holster would betray him. He waited for the marksman he could not locate to try again, watching for muzzle fire, but after five minutes of silence he called softly to Sam.

"See anything?"

A disgusted voice came back. "Nothing, Colonel, but I heard him take off like a scalded cat. Did you get hit?"

The sheriff sensed the black man approaching and kept his tone low. "No. He missed. You get to town, to the saloons. Say I'm shot bad and you're looking for Doc Combs."

Sam leaned the buffalo gun against the stair rail and went off at a run as Savage got to his feet and turned into the dark parlor, where Edna had blown out the lamp.

"John?"

Her voice held fright, not for herself but for him. It came from the hallway and he laughed shortly to reassure her.

"It's all right. You know no bullet is going to kill me."

From the same direction Verne said, "That's stupid to believe. Who was it?" His words sounded shaky.

"Take your pick, but my first guess would be Pete Slocum. I gave him until morning to clear out."

"What if he doesn't?"

"I told him I'd kill him. I will."

Hannah's breath sucked in through his

teeth. "What would happen to you?"

"Nothing."

His hands found his wife and the straining muscles of her throat told him she did not believe him. He kissed her, rubbed his nose against her as a tease.

"Go on up to bed, girl, I'll be there later. Good night, Verne."

She turned toward the stairs and Hannah fumbled his way through the door. Savage followed him to the steps, took the buffalo gun and went back inside to sit at the shattered window to listen to the night and wait for Sam. Shortly the black man whistled, signaling his coming, and walked almost silently into the room.

"Colonel? You here?"

"By the window. What did you find?"

"Pete Slocum in the Alhambra celebrating. He thinks you're dying."

"Know how long he's been there?"

The black man said sourly, "Morrison says he came in five minutes ahead of me. He could have shot at you and made it there easy. Doc Combs was in the saloon, too, and he's on his way as soon as he picks up his bag. I couldn't well head him off with everybody listening."

"We'll meet him on the way. Saddle up for me while I make up a pack and fill some canteens. Then we'll call on Mr. Slocum. You won't need a horse."

Savage handed the Sharps over, followed Sam through the house to the barn for saddlebags and canteens and left him with the gray, returning to the kitchen. He lit a table lamp, filled the bags from the food chest, pumped water, checked the loads in his revolver and put extra ammunition in a pocket. He left a note for Edna saying he would be gone a few days, then, his arms loaded, he went out through the back. Sam had the gray ready and when Savage had the gear aboard and was mounted he walked beside the sheriff along Allen, the buffalo gun balanced over his shoulder.

They met Doc Combs halfway to town and stopped to tell him why he wasn't needed, received a caustic prophecy that he expected to be called again soon enough and probably for a burial of the sheriff. Savage handed him two dollars for his trouble and rode on.

At the Alhambra he left the gray at the rail and shoved quietly ahead of Sam through the batwings. Inside the lighted room they stopped to let their eyes adjust. The saloon was in pandemonium, as though this were the Fourth of July. Slocum was buying, the loafers and barflies making him a hero at the tops of their voices for having rid them of the sheriff.

Slocum stood at the bar, his back to the doorway, head tilted to pour a mug of beer down his throat. The man beside him glanced toward the swinging louvers, nudged Pistol Pete and yelped.

"What the hell . . . he's here. Savage."

Slocum was a little drunk, but not so drunk that he did not freeze, the mug against his mouth. He dropped his eyes to the backbar mirror and spewed out the beer in his throat. Savage watched the reflection as the coarse face went slack and read the slow mind. Positioned as he was, Slocum would have to drop the mug to go for his gun, would have to turn half around to fire. He could not do it all before Savage could shoot him with the revolver already leveled on him.

Into the sudden silence the sheriff's low voice carried as if he shouted. "I told you to get out of this county."

Slocum swallowed loudly. "In the morning, you said. I got until sunup, ain't I?"

"Not since you tried to shoot me off my porch. You're going now. Don't turn. Lift your gun with two fingers and toss it behind you."

The man hesitated. "Aw, Sheriff, I didn't . . ."

"Drop it. The rest of you back away from him slow."

The men who had so recently applauded the outlaw edged both ways along the bar, leaving him isolated, their eyes wary on Sam at Savage's side sweeping the Sharps over them. Slocum's thumb and forefinger shook as he lowered his hand, pulled up his .45 and dropped it at his heels.

Savage said evenly, "Kick it over here, Sam."

The black man crossed, both hands holding the buffalo gun, and used the side of his foot to spin the short gun across the sawdust between Savage's toes, then stepped back to his side. The sheriff crouched without looking away from Slocum, felt for the gun with his left hand, straightened and tucked it into his trousers band.

"Now turn and face me, Slocum. Where's your horse?"

Pistol Pete turned with slow care, a worried frown puckering his whole face. "Around the corner, Sheriff, but I ain't got my gear on it yet. I got no water."

Savage ignored that. "Sam, bring the rope off my pommel, tie a noose, drop it over his head and walk him out. If he tries to bolt, shoot him."

Slocum lost all color, yelping. "You ain't fixing to lynch me?"

"No."

Sam backed through the door, letting the louvers flap shut. With the buffalo gun no longer threatening them a dozen .45's could have riddled Savage, but all the men were in front of him. No one made a move. Sam returned with the rope, the Sharps under his arm while he knotted the loop. He fitted it around Slocum's neck, drew it close and stepped out of reach to march the outlaw ahead of him. When they were on the sidewalk Savage measured the rigid figures before him.

"Anybody want to draw cards in the game?"

No one did. Savage backed to the door swinging the pearl-handled gun in an arc around the room. He spoke without emphasis.

"If any of you put your head outside in the next fifteen minutes it will be blown off." His next step took him through the batwings.

CHAPTER 12

Savage led the gray around the corner. Slocum was already in his saddle, his hands locked over his head and the rope taut so that it would jerk him to the ground if the horse moved. The sheriff took the Sharps to free Sam's hands and the black rider used Pistol Pete's own lariat to tie his wrists behind him and his legs to the stirrups, passing the line under the animal's belly, then took back the long gun and waited while Savage mounted.

"You take Edna to the ranch while I'm gone," the sheriff said. "I want you both out of town in case somebody gets an idea you aren't protected and thinks he can get back at me through you two."

Sam gave him a wide smile. "That's the happiest words you've said since we've been in this stinking hole. It will be fine to see the crew."

John Savage did not need to say how

much he wanted to join them and return to the San Pedro for good. He kneed the gray close to Slocum's mount, took the rope off the man's neck and cinched it over the horn. The loose end he fastened to his own pommel, then headed east out of town toward a destination he had chosen when Sam had reported the outlaw bragging in the Alhambra.

Skeleton Canyon winds through the rough Peloncillo Mountains from the Animas Valley in New Mexico to the San Simon Valley in Arizona. In the early days of Tombstone's history the Animas was headquarters territory for outlaws. Curly Bill Brocious, Ike Clanton, Dick Grey, Billy Lane all had spreads. Down in this most remote southwest corner of New Mexico there still stood remnants of their hideouts, the old Cloverleaf ranch house, the Roofless Adobe, the Double Adobe and other weather-beaten structures that had sheltered those who lived by preying on a wide area.

Skeleton was a traditional route for smugglers' trains winding out of Mexico by way of San Luis Pass through the Animas range and across the valley, following the canyon gorges where the wild silence was broken only by the mule bells echoing off the red cliffs. Two separate murderous encounters between the smugglers and the outlaws bent on raiding the trains had left masses of macabre detritus on the rocky floor, bodies of many men killed there and never buried. Scavenging animals and birds had cleaned the bones and most still lay in a white scatter like a game of toss sticks, a charnel place known as the Devil's Graveyard. Many had been washed away by flood waters of the creek and others had been gathered as souvenirs.

It was a good fifty miles from Tombstone to the Skeleton and every mile had been marked by bloodshed, but the whole district was empty now and very little traffic moved through it. John Savage was in no hurry, walking the gray through the night and the next day, trailing Slocum on the lead line, pausing periodically to rest and water the horses and his prisoner, dismounting him for the sake of the animal but leaving the wrists tied.

At such a stop just past the last branch of the trail where the Skeleton Canyon fork turned south, Pistol Pete, almost asleep in the hot afternoon, roused and became aware of where Savage was headed and yelled, the first sound he had made since leaving town.

"Don't take me to that canyon, man. My God, no."

Savage, taking the rope off his legs, looked up without expression. "Why not? You'll have lots of company."

Slocum shook as if he had ague when the sheriff lifted him down. His legs gave way and he crumpled to the ground and sat, rolling his eyes.

"I don't want to die. Most of all not there. I was with some boys that hit a bunch of smugglers bringing up a herd we wanted. One of the Mex was still alive when we went in and put a curse on me before I finished him off. He said I'd die there too and the devil would come for me and burn me in hell. Sheriff, please. Don't let that happen."

Savage rinsed his mouth with water and held the canteen for Slocum's short drink. "I don't put any stock in superstition. One life is enough."

He attended to the horses, rested for fifteen minutes, ignoring Slocum's raving pleas, then mounted him and bound him and led him on down the southern track. When they reached the bone-strewn area he got down, tied the horses to a scrub bush, pulled Slocum out of the saddle, cut his wrists free and stepped in front of the outlaw where he sat drumming his numbed feet on the ground.

"Rub some circulation into your hands."

They had been bound for many hours and were white, bloodless. Slocum held them in front of him, unable at once to flex the fingers.

"Damn you, Savage, if I had my gun . . ."

"You will have it. When you can use it."

A spark of hope leaped to the man's eyes. "You're going to give me a chance to draw against you?"

"Get your blood going."

Slocum went to work at it, rubbing the pale palms together, trying to bend one finger at a time, rocking as pain began to replace the loss of feeling. The fire in his hands became excruciating.

"It hurts. Jesus it hurts."

"Take it slow. We've got time."

It took an hour while the outlaw grimaced and sweat stood in large drops on his face. Gradually color returned and at length the hands were limber. Savage stood away in case Pistol Pete decided to jump him. Watching the man's eyes, he felt for the gun in his belt, broke it, felt over the chambers and found them filled, and returned the gun to the belt.

He backed to the horses, mounted the gray, tossed clear the lead line he had looped over his pommel and backed both animals along the edge of the stream bed.

In the wet season the creek ran bank full. Now it was parched, the bottom caked and laced with a web of deep cracks.

Aghast, Pete Slocum cried out, "You ain't going to leave me this way? What about my gun? My chance?"

Savage continued backing. Slocum began to run after him. The sheriff drew the pearl-handled weapon.

"Stay put, Pete. Your chance is coming."

The outlaw stopped, his clawed hands outstretched while Savage moved the horses out of short gun range. There he lifted Slocum's .45, held it up for the man to see, then flung it away into a cluster of rocks and called:

"When you get thirsty enough use that."

He wheeled the gray, spurred it and towed the second horse back along the trail. Over his shoulder he saw Pistol Pete Slocum running to paw among the stones to find his gun.

Savage rode over the rise ahead until he was beyond Slocum's sight, reined in there and sat listening, wondering which choice the outlaw would take. In the hot sun he could not walk far without water and there was none within his range. Would he tenaciously stumble around the desert until he dropped? Or not?

A shriek came. High and drawn out, as long as the breath for it lasted, in raging anguish. Then the shot. Slocum knew the country and that thirst was a hard way to die. This much was finished.

Savage rode back to where Pistol Pete's body lay twisted on the rocks, the gun fallen close beside him. The sheriff stepped down, made certain the outlaw was dead, shoved the .45 back under his belt. Working deliberately, he stripped the corpse, made a bundle of the clothes and tied it by the belt on Slocum's horse, then swung up and rode five miles to where a clump of greasewood was rooted among a mound of boulders. He cut the brush that would burn hot and fast, piled it under and on top of the bundle, set it afire and waited while flames crackled and ate through the cloth and leather. When only ash was left he scattered those, sweeping through them with a branch, and finally gathered the metal bits, added the outlaw's gun and rolled a large stone over them. When he finished he rode toward Tombstone until dark, then made a camp, ate from the saddlebag and rolled in his blanket and slept well through the night.

When he reached water and grass he took the head gear and saddle off Slocum's horse, buried those and slapped the animal free.

As he rode into the corral at Tombstone, Hal Hawser, the county attorney, walked out of the saddle shop next door. He stepped in front of Savage, stopping him.

"What did you do with him?"

The sheriff said indifferently, "With who?"

"Pete Slocum. You took him out of town with a rope around his neck. Tell me and tell it straight or I'll yank you before a grand jury and have you indicted for murder."

Savage's smile was thin, his eyes hooded. He drew the pearl-handled gun, tossed it once in his palm and extended it down toward the attorney.

"Smell it. It hasn't been fired. And I didn't hang him. Don't you need a body before you ask for an indictment?"

The lawyer stepped back from the proffered weapon, scowling. "Oil and a rag clean a gun. And I'll find the body."

The sheriff swung down. "Good luck looking for it. Pete's gone to Mexico and I don't think he means to come back."

He walked around the man, taking the gray into the runway to unsaddle and groom, brushing the hide leisurely. He had no fear that Pete Slocum's remains would be located in any recognizable condition.

Already the flesh would be eaten away and the bones scattered and very shortly the Arizona sun would have bleached them to match the many others strewn along the canyon trail. Pistol Pete would lie unnoticed surrounded by his own kind.

CHAPTER 13

Bobby Burch reported that Tombstone had been uneasily quiet during the sheriff's short absence. There had been no robberies, no saloon brawls. The only excitement had been after Savage herded Pete Slocum out of town when the toughs for whom the outlaw had been buying drinks had further fortified themselves, building to a vengeful mood, and then shot up the street. There was no one else downtown and a few more windows had been broken but no greater damage done. Burch had blown out the lamps and sat out the half hour of fireworks in the dark office.

It was too bad, the sheriff said dryly, that they had not hit each other. So the example of Pistol Pete Slocum had been lost on the rowdies and the job was not over. He made a foot patrol to test the present temper and met no challenge, only sullen glares.

The hostler lost no time in spreading the

news of Hal Hawser's threat of a murder indictment, and in the morning the population rode out as a posse with the attorney to look for Slocum's body.

John Savage took the opportunity, while the streets should be at peace, to go to the ranch for his wife and Sam. It twisted a knife in him to cross the green acres, and when the headquarters buildings were in sight his eyes searched the structures and fences for signs of disrepair, but there was nothing to complain of. Bo Roberts was on top of it. Roundup was finished, the crew returned and busy with routine chores.

The old easiness was not in their greeting; there was a reserve, as though he were a visiting stranger when they gathered in the cookhouse, except that Roberts showed a sympathetic interest, questioning the Colonel about his progress.

Savage did not mention Slocum, only shook his head when the foreman said Sam had told him the sheriff had taken the outlaw somewhere.

"Nothing for you to bother thinking about, Bo. You've got your hands full here."

He spent the afternoon listening to Roberts detail the success of the roundup, the increase of calves, the work that was being done at headquarters. He knew a keen jealousy that he was not part of it all, felt almost an outsider. But when night came he luxuriated in his own bed in his own room and his own house with Edna, where they ought to be.

The short stay had brought back her laughter, which came so seldom in town, and the crew treated her with the warmth they always had, for which he was grateful. She was not ostracized because of his damned star. Sam drove her back to town in the buggy while Savage, savoring her fresh pleasure, rode the gray at her side.

By the time they reached town the posse had returned empty-handed. They had not even found Pete Slocum's horse, wherever it had wandered. As the days passed the outlaw's disappearance became less talked of and Tombstone settled down in some degree. Savage watched for some repercussion from the Tucson Ring but those politicians were apparently looking the other way, unwilling to bring it to attention that they had not been able to protect their hireling.

Three loafers left voluntarily. The saddlery had been broken into and three newly finished saddles taken. John Savage went looking for the riders and within two weeks brought back the gear loaded on a tow horse, but the loafers did not return. Savage then rousted the rest of the group that hung around the benches before the saddlery and the photography shop next door.

This time the commissioners made no protest and even Horace Simpson kept silent and did not demand the sheriff's badge. There was no further immediate trouble.

Edna Savage's spirits remained higher than they had been. She had dreaded the danger her husband faced hourly but as time dragged on and there were no more attempts on him and the town stayed quiet she began to believe his job was nearing its end. Then Savage noted a growing edginess in her. For the first time she appeared worried about her brother who Bobby Burch reported was still gambling, even more heavily, and still losing.

The sheriff puzzled over what he might do about Verne Hannah. He considered facing the young man with an ultimatum but discarded the idea. If Edna herself was beginning to be concerned about the losses he might succeed only in reversing that development, make her withdraw to a blanket defense of her brother.

Three nights in a row Savage came home for supper to find his brother-in-law already in the kitchen helping with the preparations and knew from the distress in his wife's eyes that Verne was again asking for money. For the first time in his life the sheriff was at a loss to find a solution to a problem, yet he kept his own counsel. There was no one he felt at liberty to discuss the situation with, certainly not Bobby Butch or Old Sam. There was Lew Trumble, his old rider, but it gorged him to think of seeming to ask advice of the commissioner. The only power he really held in his job was in keeping his independence, not explaining himself, keeping everyone off balance, being invulnerable. If Bo Roberts were in town Savage might have talked it over with the foreman, but Roberts was at the Lazy S and showed no indication that he would ever come to Tombstone.

So the weeks stretched out. Aside from an occasional arrest of an obstreperous drunk Savage had little call to exercise his legal authority. A resolution grew in Savage. Tax time was upon them and if the town was still quiet when that was finished he would resign and take his wife home where she was not so handy for being milked by Verne. That could not come too soon to suit him.

Bobby Burch was spending most of his time away from the office riding from one outlying ranch to another to collect money due both the county and the territory. Collections were slow. Cochise County had lost two thirds of its business when the mines closed. There was no use trying to levy on the unproductive, waterlogged shafts. Reading the delinquency rolls, John Savage read the death notice of Tombstone whether or not Lew Trumble and the commissioners believed it. Still, there were pockets where people and businesses prospered and Juan Soto was among these.

Soto claimed a Spanish descent but to John Savage he looked Mexican Indian. Bobby Burch called him to the sheriff's attention after a tax collection trip.

"That fellow over in Contention, I can't figure him out. He always has money to buy drinks for anybody in the saloon and he doesn't mind who he entertains or how much they drink. The camp isn't that rich anymore."

There was a good deal of whiskey on the deputy's breath. Savage said wryly, "He'll buy for a tax collector even? What do you know about him?"

"Nobody seems to know much. They say he comes from California. If he's rich I don't see why he stays in Contention."

The place was one of the satellite camps that had grown up around Tombstone in the San Pedro Valley. It had been a mill town in its heyday but had shrunk to little more than a ghost town, certainly an odd location for an up-and-coming businessman to make his headquarters. Savage had seen the man in the Tombstone gambling houses but during his term of office he had heard no reports of trouble in what was left of the mill camp to take him there.

Now Burch's comments made him curious. Not being one to take another man's word at face value, the sheriff rode out to Contention to see for himself. He found Soto at a card table in the only saloon remaining open, wearing American clothes and a flat-brimmed Mexican hat from which some twenty silver pesos dangled, twinkling. The half-dozen men around the five players were laughing, joking, Juan Soto obviously enjoying himself as the center of attention. They fell silent when the man with the badge walked in.

Savage touched a finger to his hat in salute, had a single drink at the bar and left, frowning that the bartender had refused his payment, indicating Soto as his host. The sheriff nodded thanks on his way out, not wanting to rouse suspicion that he was there for any reason other than refreshment.

He stepped unhurriedly up to his saddle

and walked the gray through a street more moribund than any in Tombstone. He had no information against Soto. The tax rolls identified him as owner of the feed store, the livery and the dilapidated hotel. But Savage had an instinct that there was more behind that surface. The man was wrong.

As there always had been, there was some rustling in the valley, but less in the vicinity of Contention than elsewhere. The sheriff had nothing to connect Juan Soto with the thievery, but if he were head of a ring he would logically keep his operations at a distance from his home base. Savage decided to keep closer attention on the pattern of the stealing. Of necessity he had neglected that aspect of outlawry because of the time involved in trying to run down a stolen animal, and had concentrated on policing Tombstone proper where he had assumed the rustling originated. But perhaps that was not entirely so.

During the next two weeks four complaints came in about the disappearance of horses, two single animals, two of pairs and one man had lost six. The sheriff investigated each claim. Neither he nor the owners could find any trace of tracks to tell which way the thieves had gone. But one thing shone clear. The animals had been taken from points on a wide circle with Contention at its center. Yet Savage could not bring in Juan Soto on suspicion alone.

While he debated how to trap the man a rider brought word that two cattle buyers had been ambushed on their way south from the Benson rail station in a rented rig. Savage and Burch rode out to see.

The bodies lay twisted off the side of the road, guarded by a Mexican sheep herder who with the messenger had discovered them. Both men had been shot through the back of the head. The buggy lay on its side near them with the corpse of the horse still in the shattered traces. Savage dismounted for a closer examination. All the pockets had been turned out, and the larger man, later identified as Oscar Tully from Denver, had a leather pouch handcuffed to one wrist. The side of the pouch had been slashed and it was empty. The ground around Tully was trampled with boot prints but there was nothing significant about the soles that had made them.

Savage lifted the arm, which was already stiffening, and a bit of bright metal winked at him from the dust. The sheriff picked up a polished Mexican silver peso and turned it in his fingers. A small hole was bored near its edge and three links of a fine silver chain were attached there, the free link spread and twisted as if it had been violently torn from its fastening. The sheriff closed his eyes, visualizing Juan Soto's hat and the coins sparkling around the brim edge. He tried to recall what they had hung on but could not except that they had swung free, not stiffly. Savage whistled a note too low for the others to hear and straightened, closing his palm around the hot coin, looking from the messenger to the herder.

"This is how you found them? You didn't move anything?"

"Nothing, señor." The Mexican was emphatic. "Ronnie Carter here warned me to stay back, only keep animals away."

"Good." Savage gave each a dollar. "I'll send a wagon from Benson for them. Wait until it comes." He climbed back to his saddle, jerking his head for Burch to follow.

From the Benson liveryman they learned who the cattle buyers had been and that Tully had had to hold the leather bag in both hands while he got into the rig. It had appeared very heavy. Beyond that he could tell nothing. Savage thanked him, stepped the gray out of hearing distance and told his deputy:

"Find someone to bring in those bodies, then go back to the office and stay there."

163

Bobby Burch raised his brows. "Where are you going?"

"Contention. To see Juan Soto." He showed the peso with the chain.

"Alone?" The deputy did not approve.

Savage rode away without an answer. Soto sat at the table where the sheriff had seen him on his first visit, king of the hill with laughing courtiers around him. Again a silence fell. Savage angled past the table to the bar, asked for beer and made no attempt to pay for it. With one foot on the brass rail and an elbow on the counter, he watched the mirror as the men began relaxing. There was a gap in the evenly spaced circle of coins around Soto's hat brim.

The man could certainly have murdered and robbed the cattle buyers alone, but had he? From the number of footprints around the scene Savage thought not. It seemed more likely that others in the saloon had been with him, that at least some of them made up a band of predators in the old style of outlawry that had scourged the territory in the boom days. The sheriff took his time, impressing the faces of all of them on his mind. He would not forget them.

They were all Mexican or Indian, low-browed, evil-looking. Even if Savage could take Juan Soto out of this company now he could not make the ride to Tombstone with the leader without coming under a mass attack. He would have to use a different tactic, one that required time, for he wanted not only Soto himself but the gang as well. Saying nothing, he went out to the gray and rode toward his town.

What he needed was an informer within the group and that meant a man from south of the border. Savage had many on his ranch crew but they were simple cow hands and would be more apt than not to betray themselves and be murdered. He knew only one person capable of handling such a chore. If he would. And it galled Savage to go hat in hand to him. But he had always faced what he had to squarely and he went straight to the Suzie Golff house and twisted the bell.

Mario Valdez opened the door, his black eyes widening in surprise, then narrowing on the sheriff's star. He did not speak.

Savage said, "May I come in? I need to talk to you and Rosa."

The rider stepped back and trailed Savage into the parlor, calling his wife from the kitchen. The Opata woman saw Savage and ran to him with a happy cry, catching his hand in both of hers.

"The Colonel, Mario. He comes to us

again. Are we all going home now?"

Savage felt a twinge of guilt at going through a woman, but as he paid heed to Edna so Mario might listen to his wife when he would listen to no one else. He put his hands on her shoulders.

"I have much need of Mario, Rosa. Only he can help me solve a big trouble. Will you both listen?"

He told them about the murder of the cattle buyers and the theft of their gold, dangled the Soto peso and told where he had found it. He described his visit to the Contention saloon and the gang he had seen there.

"I need Mario because he can think and is a Mexican. I want him to join that gang and learn all he can about them so I can stop them."

Mario's laugh was hard. "Me? Spy for a sheriff? In a pig's eye, Colonel. I'm not as crazy as you."

Savage did not look toward him, his eyes on Rosa's. "Think about this, Mario. Your people don't like the way the Anglos look down on Mexicans but men like Juan Soto and his crowd give them good reason. They give you a bad name your honest kind do not deserve. Are you going to let them get away with rustling, robbery, murder and not lift your hand in your own defense? I thought you had pride."

Mario's breath hissed in. He stood blazing for a second, flung about, stalked to the door and yanked it open. "Don't be here when I come back." The wall rattled when he slammed the panel after him.

Rosa Valdez frowned after him, sighed, dropped her eyes and hurried back to the kitchen. John Savage went out more quietly than Valdez, the taste of defeat like bile in his mouth.

He was silent, withdrawn, through supper that evening, thankful only that Verne had not appeared, not certain he could have sat through the meal with him. Afterward he sat in the parlor reading the weekly paper and kneading his thigh while his wife crocheted an afghan square. Usually if she gave him time he would tell her what troubled him, but this night it seemed that he would not.

She said very softly, "Can't you talk about it to me, John?"

He crumpled the paper, dropped it and looked at her over the half glass of the steel-rimmed spectacles he used for reading, being very far-sighted. He spoke in short sentences, forcing control of his voice, telling her about the day and his appeal to

Mario and the rider's blunt refusal.

"I am sorry." Edna put the work aside and brought him coffee laced with whiskey, strong enough to relax him and let him sleep. "There'll be another way. Sometime you'll find Soto alone, and maybe without him the others will make mistakes, brag about some crime where it will get back to you. It may take time."

How much time, he wondered, and knew he could not leave the sheriff's position until he cleaned out this nest of killers.

In the morning Savage sent Bobby Burch on patrol and sat in the empty office wondering how he could tempt Juan Soto into the open with not too many men around him. At eight-thirty Mario Valdez drove Horace Simpson's wife and homely daughter past the window for a shopping trip. Ten minutes later Mario, wearing the hot woolen suit the banker had stuck him with, walked into the office, reversed the chair across from Savage and straddled it, folding his arms on the back, his face bleak.

"You and Rosa. You play foul. Last night she locked me out of the bedroom. Said she wouldn't sleep with a coward or a mule. So I'm here. What do I do?"

"Thanks, Mario." Savage did not crow. "It took courage for you to come. Get some comfortable clothes and spend your free time in Contention. First, take Soto's fancy coin to him and say you picked it up where the buyers were killed and knew he'd want it back so it didn't turn up in the wrong hands. From then on throw money around in the saloon. I'll give it to you. Brag that you have plenty and know where a lot more is hidden."

Mario looked thoughtful. "Where is it supposed to come from?"

"A stage robbery pulled years ago by Johnny Ringo. There was such a robbery. Soto can look it up if he wants. Ringo was identified but the money was never found. Soto will want that cache for himself so I think he'll play along, try to ace himself in with you to get at it. At least long enough for you to find out who the others are and what all they're involved in. It will be dangerous."

Valdez eyed the sheriff morosely. "Everything I ever did for you was dangerous. And what you're doing behind that badge is plain suicide."

Savage took the inference as meaning that Mario, though he resented to the marrow working for the law, would not refuse a challenge less than the Colonel was facing daily. A vast relief lightened the morning for him.

"There's something else I want, hard evidence against Soto, which I won't find in Tombstone. Aside from that coin he's too careful. I need a photograph to send to California to learn what record he has there. We'll go get a camera from Luke Mullen and have him teach you to use it. That will help explain why a family man with a steady job doesn't do his card playing here where he lives. Mullen has a corner on the Tombstone photography market and doesn't want competition." Savage stood up. "We'll take the alley to the shop so no one spots us going in there together, and Luke will keep his mouth shut."

CHAPTER 14

John Savage did not see Mario Valdez to speak to for ten days. The Mexican was around town driving the Simpson carriage but on his off time he disappeared. When a week had passed Luke Mullen slipped into the sheriff's office with an envelope. The photographer had been glad to co-operate with the sheriff and to keep his mouth closed. He had had a rise in business since the toughs were no longer hanging around his doorway.

"Your new boy brought in some plates yesterday," he said and dropped an envelope on the desk. "I printed two sets. He took one with him and here's the other."

Savage shook out six photographs and a note listing five names, men, Mario wrote, who were the core of Juan Soto's gang, who had taken part in the murder of the cattle buyers. The portraits were not the most professional but they were recognizable. The five henchmen were hatless, grinning in the sunshine before the Contention saloon. Soto's bespangled hat was shoved to the back of his head and did not shadow his face.

"Good enough, Luke," the sheriff said. "Make me up another sixty copies of each as soon as you can."

The photographer caught his breath. "That's going to cost you pretty, John . . . Sheriff."

Savage was dry. "I can stand it if it's worth it."

When the man had left the sheriff sat writing letters to the authorities of every California county asking for information they might have of any of the men in the enclosed pictures. The next day he took the envelopes to Benson to mail.

In the blackness before dawn of the tenth night after Mario Valdez had first gone to Contention, John Savage waked to a sharp rattling against the window glass. He rose quietly so he would not wake Edna but did not go near the frame he could not see. Someone was throwing gravel and it was probably not a friendly visitor. He pulled his trousers on over his nightshirt, drew the pearl-handled gun from the holster and padded barefoot down the stairs. Easing the front door open, he crossed the porch, descended to the dusty yard and walked without sound to the corner of the house. From there he smelled a sweated horse and heard its snort as it blew. It had been run hard. He waited until he could make out a dim figure. One hand was stretched up as if it held the rein close to the bit. The other scooped up gravel and threw it toward the second floor. There was no evidence of a rifle or shotgun.

With only his head protruding from the corner so his white nightshirt was behind the wall, Savage called sharply:

"Who is it?"

"Boss? Colonel?" The voice was Mario's but sounded mushy.

"Come in the house."

Savage waited where he was until Mario brought the horse forward and tied it to the porch rail, then led him into the parlor, pulled the curtains over the new glass of the front window, felt for the table lamp and lighted it. When he turned Mario Valdez stood slumped against the closed door, gradually sinking toward the floor. Savage jumped for him, caught him under the arms and half-carried him to a chair beside the table.

As the flame on the wick came up a grunt burst from the sheriff as if he had taken a stomach punch. Mario's hair was matted with blood, his face streaked with it and swollen, one eye closed and his mouth pulped. His arms hung limp at his sides. Savage crossed to the lowboy for a brandy decanter and glass. The liquor would burn but it would help. He held the glass to Mario's thickened lips, dribbling the liquid through them.

"Soto?" He spoke only the name.

Valdez nodded, took the glass and emptied it, held it out for more. When Savage had refilled it the Mexican tossed the brandy back with a show of more strength.

"After the Ringo money?" Savage guessed. He was raging at himself. He should have been more explicit, told Mario to agree to show the killer a location, then report to him so he could be waiting. But he had not spelled it out.

Mario filled his lungs and sat straighter. "That's better. The money, yes. I got Soto aside and said I'd show him where it was and we'd split. He got drunk and shot off his mouth. When he passed out the others grabbed me, took me to the woodshed and whaled me to make me tell them. I took all I wanted to make it look right, then caved, said I'd show them if they'd let me alone, let me sleep off the damage." He paused and Savage poured him another drink. After that the rider tried a painful smile. "The damn fools bit. They're a stupid lot sober and with whiskey in them they're worse. They locked me in the shed. I dug out with a spur and rode in. What's next?"

John Savage was shocked that his old horse breaker was ready to go on. "For you, nothing. You did your job. With a vengeance."

"Vengeance sounds good, Colonel. I'll never put on a badge, but I want a crack at that crowd when you're ready." He got up and walked steadily through the door.

In the following days answers to his letters began arriving for the sheriff of Cochise County. Word came from San Bernardino that Soto, under the name Martinez, had commanded a gang of stage and train robbers and had left town a half jump ahead of a lynch mob, but there was no killing involved. Other messages filtered in, all negative. Then San Francisco responded with what Savage had hoped to learn. Soto was known in the bay city as Juan Gomez, leader of a band of highwaymen who the year previously had killed an army paymaster, but the man had positively identified Gomez before he died. No one though had any records on the men in the other five photographs, so those must be local Arizona border toughs.

When Bobby Burch came in from patrol near five o'clock Savage had hidden the California letters under a sheaf of papers in the bottom desk drawer. Bobby was too much a gossip to trust in this development.

The sheriff told him, "Tomorrow ride to Contention on your tax rounds. Catch Juan Soto alone and tell him that Mario Valdez wants to meet him at midnight in the O.K. Corral, by himself. And Bobby, if you whisper a word to anyone I'll have your hide nailed to this door. Believe me."

Burch blinked back. "But I've already collected from Contention."

The sheriff flattened both palms on the desk and half-rose from the chair, his eyes like obsidian. "If you want to keep this job, do as I tell you. Good night."

Steaming, Savage left the deputy in the office and on his way home detoured by the Suzie Golff house to alert Mario.

"When Soto comes, meet him in front of the first stall. Tell him you're ready to take him to the gold, to wait until you saddle, then fade back. I'll be in the stall to take him and I don't want you where he can shoot you if he decides to draw."

It worked like a charm. Mario stood in

the lantern light of the runway and Juan Soto rode toward him, his brim coins dancing and winking, calling as he saw the figure:

"Amigo, you ran away from me. I thought I would have to come for you to take our ride."

Valdez snarled convincingly, "You're damn right I ran. Your pals beat me up trying to cut in. Get down and rest your back side while I saddle."

He retreated, watching the outlaw dismount. As Soto stepped out of his saddle, while one hand hung on to the horn and the other the rein, John Savage came noiselessly from the stall. Before Soto's foot touched the runway straw the sheriff's gun prodded against the killer's spine.

"Just like that. Come down with your hands high and keep them up."

Soto froze midway. Mario Valdez yelped as if in shocked surprise, spun and dived through the rear doorway into the night. Silently Savage complimented him on the act. It should throw off Soto's suspicion of a trap, for since Mario had kept a chilly distance from the Colonel in town there was nothing to associate them with each other.

Savage found a sheathed knife at the back of Soto's neck, dropped it in a pocket, emptied the man's holster and took another knife from his boot top. He cuffed the hands behind the back and marched him, protesting, to the jail. With the cell grille and the office door locked, he carried a shotgun back to the livery, saddled the gray and rode for Contention. Half a mile outside Tombstone the sheriff heard hoofs drumming behind him, reined off the road and waited in the dense dark beside a greasewood clump. Shortly the starlight showed him Mario Valdez approaching and he kneed his horse into sight, keeping his voice dry.

"You're riding late."

Valdez' tone was light. "So are you, Colonel, but they'll still be at the saloon. They spend all night there and sleep days. I want my crack at them too."

Neither said anything more. Savage was pleased to have his old rider with him because he did not know how many men he was going to face. The glow through the saloon door was the only light in camp when they left the horses at the rail, well separated from the clutch of other animals there.

"Take the rear," Savage said.

He gave Valdez time to reach the back, took off his hat and looked over the batwings. Only the five hard-core gang members were in the room. There was no one behind the bar and Savage assumed that Soto owned this place as well as his other enterprises. He pushed through fast, the shotgun parting the louvers ahead of him, and stepped aside, putting his back against the wall.

"Sit tight and listen." The flat, hard voice carried through the room. "Bob Ellis is dead. Pete Slocum is gone and so are some other Tombstone trash. They won't be back. It's your turn. If you're still in Cochise County at daylight you'll never leave it."

Savage backed halfway through the swinging doors, raised the shotgun and fired at the lamp hanging above the table, let the louvers flap and dodged along the sidewalk beyond the outlaws' horses. He heard yells as the glass bowl of the lamp shattered and flaming oil splattered over the men beneath. There was the grating of chairs, then running feet. The rear door slammed open. A short gun beyond it exploded twice and two high cries followed. The remaining feet reversed direction and charged for the front. Three men, their clothes burning, erupted through the entrance slapping at the flames, flung themselves on horses and drove into the night. Inside, the tinder dry wood of table, chairs, flooring flared up and fire roiled to fill the room with red malignancy.

Savage untied the two remaining horses, slapped them out of danger, mounted the frightened, dancing gray and took Mario's animal beyond the perimeter of heat and brilliance. Mario came running along the side of the building where the sun-cured walls were beginning to buckle, the shiplap boards curling into red and black ribbons. Mario chased his horse in a circle as it fought the rein to bolt, stepped astride, broke his gun, blew down the barrel and holstered it. Then the two headed home, alert for ambush.

CHAPTER 15

John Savage felt secure that with the evidence of Soto's identification as a murderer from San Francisco and Mario Valdez' testimony that the outlaw had bragged about waylaying the cattle buyers to kill and rob them made a case so strong that even Judge Ben South would have to convict and sentence him either to hang or a life term in prison.

He took Mario to the county attorney to tell his story and he exhibited the San Francisco letter. Hal Hawser was sufficiently impressed to secure an indictment and empanel a grand jury and take Soto before the circuit rider when he came through Tombstone the following month, and even Judge Malcomb denied bail.

But shortly before the trial Bobby Burch brought Savage word that Jack Seers and Benson Hodges of the Tucson Ring had made a surreptitious visit to Tombstone. He had not discovered their presence until he met them in a rig on the Benson road headed for the railroad. By then it was too late.

The trial lasted three days. Hawser made a strong case for the prosecution, putting Mario Valdez on the stand. The defense called witness after witness, hangers-on of the Contention saloon who all swore that Juan Soto had not left the card table for the twenty-four hours during which the two cattle buyers had been killed. Judge Ben South advised the jurors that what Valdez said he had been told by the outlaws was hearsay and not admissible. The verdict was not guilty again.

Seeing how it would go, John Savage waited only until Mario had finished his testimony and took him out to the street. He kept all feeling out of his face and voice.

"Now that you've spoken against Soto you're marked if he goes free. You'll have to take Rosa and the kids and disappear. Mario, you've done this much for me, go back to the Lazy S. He doesn't connect you with that. Stay there at least until I get rid of him."

The Mexican kicked at the dust. "What about you, Colonel? You know you're being ridiculed the same as always. Why don't you toss that star in the trash and come home too? I'd look a fool if I went back there with you still wearing that damned thing."

"You'd look alive. You always did your own thinking, do it now. The fool's way is to box yourself in with that old obsession. You know Bo Roberts needs you with horse-breaking time coming up, and that means I need you there."

Valdez continued arguing for half an hour but he hated Simpson's cast-off clothes, he hated the banker and his wife and daughter, he hated the town life and finally, for the protection of his own family he said, he gave in. Before Juan Soto was released Mario quit his job and took his delighted wife and children back to the adobe.

Also before Soto was turned loose John Savage went to Contention and burned the remainder of the outlaw's holdings. He camped in the brush and waited two days until the killer and his retinue rode in and had grim satisfaction watching the consternation as they discovered the camp in ashes. One and then another of Soto's fringe followers drifted off until he was alone on the street shouting curses and threats against the Tombstone sheriff. Savage put the gray toward him at a walk and Soto, blinded with his fury, did not see him until he fired a shot that kicked up a spurt of dirt just in front of the outlaw's horse.

"Reach," he called. "The next one is for you."

Soto was half turned away. He wheeled to face Savage, slapping at his thigh, but stopped his hand before the draw and kicked his horse nose to nose with the gray, scarlet-faced, shouting:

"I'll kill you, you bastard. I was tried fair and acquitted. You got no call to . . ."

"By a bribed jury." Savage's words hit like a fist. "Ride out and don't show up again if you want to stay alive. You have two minutes and I won't tell you a second time."

Soto blustered, swore, but when John Savage counted "One" he reared his animal, swung away and raced eastward crosscountry, not taking the road.

Savage heard nothing more of the man for four months, but he would not let Mario Valdez bring his family back to town yet. Tombstone itself was quieter than it had ever been, though there continued to be outbreaks of crime in other parts of the county. Then Sulphur Springs Valley had a series of close-spaced robberies. One included the killing of a man and his wife with a wagon heading for town on a shopping trip they made every quarter of a year. They were shot in the backs of their heads, the man's money belt rifled and dropped beside his body.

That was close enough to Juan Soto's pattern to send John Savage out to investigate. He used four days visiting each isolated ranch and on the fourth rode into the yard of a place that had been abandoned for two years.

There was a single horse in the corral as Savage approached. He stopped outside the pole fence to look over the caving buildings. Juan Soto came out of the leaning barn within twenty feet of the sheriff, arms loaded with saddle and blanket roll. Seeing Savage, he turned to duck back out of sight, but the ranchman's braided and oiled rope was faster, settling around Soto's upper arms, pinning them to his sides, pulling him off his feet. Unable to draw, the outlaw lay quiet, his dark eyes hypnotized on the gun Savage held in his hand. The sheriff snubbed the loose rope end on his saddle horn and the gray would keep the same tension on it that it would on a thrown steer. He stepped down and stripped the man of his arsenal.

"I told you to leave the county. That includes this valley. You should have listened."

Soto's brown face blotched pale. "All

right, all right. I was just getting ready to go."

"Sure you were. You're too late for that so I'll take you out. Get on your feet and saddle up."

Savage loosened the rope, raised it and pulled it close again around the outlaw's neck, took the free end off the horn and followed Soto into the corral, keeping the line taut as the man worked with the horse. When Soto was mounted Savage tied him and towed him toward Skeleton Canyon. The place had served his purpose once and should again.

When they reached the spot where Pistol Pete Slocum's white bones lay scattered the sheriff repeated the routine, lifted Soto down, took off the ropes and gave him time to restore his circulation. Soto did not like the prospect ahead but he did not whine.

"You want me dead? You've got a gun, so get it over with. Why should I go through the hell of starting my blood pumping?"

"I want it that way."

Savage backed off from the rock where Soto sat, tied the animals, lit two Mexican cigars and put one between the outlaw's lips, threw the man's gun as far as he could, then sat down at a distance to watch Soto claw at his hands and feet. Soto looked after his gun and Savage could follow the thoughts that burned in the eyes, thoughts of how he could reach the weapon before he was shot.

They had been there half an hour and Soto's fingers were nearly flexible enough to pull a trigger. Then a shadow sped over the ground between them. Looking up, Savage saw an eagle with a five-foot wing span soar over them, its head cocked to the side to study the men, its talons curled, as large as the sheriff's hands. He judged it to be a female with a nest somewhere in the crags above and drew his gun, ready for an attack. He had heard of such birds clawing out the eyes of an unarmed man, and tension knotted his muscles.

Both he and Soto sat still except that the outlaw's head turned, following the pattern of soaring. Savage chose to keep track of her position by watching his prisoner, not risking a possible rush when his eyes were turned to the sky. He knew that she circled, sweeping lower with each pass, and when she dropped to within ten feet of their heads he fired a shot designed to miss her. She screamed, swooped into his vision and with a mighty flap of wing fans climbed nearly vertically, found an updraft and wheeled away. As the talons had reached down in her last dive Soto had clasped his arms over his face and bent double, quickly enough to prove his recovery. Savage stood up, relaxing.

"She's gone and I'm leaving now. Stay where you are until I'm over that hill, then you can find your gun. I'd advise you against trying to walk out without water."

Soto straightened, his mouth stretched in a snarl, cursing Savage in border Spanish, the voice rising higher as the sheriff backed to the horses and led them over the rise, facing the outlaw until he was out of sight.

Tying the horses again, Savage waited. Time dragged out, five minutes, ten, fifteen. It was taking Soto longer than it had Slocum to make his choice. The sheriff had about decided the man would not kill himself until thirst drove him to it when the shot split the eerie stillness.

His mouth widening to a thin, hard line, John Savage mounted the gray, left Soto's horse and rode down. He did not see the body. But he had thrown the gun into a cluster of boulders and he thought Soto must have fallen between or behind those large enough to conceal him so he turned his horse out of the trace and rode closer.

The last thing Savage expected was a second shot. It came from a rockburst on the opposite side of the road just as he reached those where he had thrown the gun. Lead slammed into Savage's left shoulder and drove him out of the saddle.

The gray shied, throwing the rider among the boulders where he lay half hidden and stunned. He did not try to move while he gasped to recover his breath, and that alone saved his life. He heard Soto's boots scraping on rock as he came out of hiding for a better look at the fallen sheriff. He took the still, sprawled figure for dead and turned, his gun in his hand, to catch up the gray.

Savage saw him, drew and fired. He lay on the injured shoulder and the movement to reach his gun sent pain stabbing deep but the bullet went through the side of Soto's chest to the heart. Savage lay where he was while waves of nausea rose through him. After fifteen minutes they subsided somewhat and he used a boulder to help drag himself to his feet. The whole side of his shirt was blood-soaked, he was weak and dizzy. He staggered toward the gray but the shots and their echoes had spooked it and it danced away. His mouth was too dry to whistle the animal to him. All he could do was sit down and wait for the horse to calm, and that took half an hour.

Finally it walked to him, head down, and

nuzzled at the sheriff's hat as though in apology. The blood smell made it nervous but it stood, trembling, while Savage, his jaw muscles bunched against pain, fumbled into the saddle. He gave no thought to stripping Soto and burning the clothes as he had after Slocum's death. It was thirty miles to the nearest ranch and he was light-headed and would need all the strength he had left to ride that far. He drank from his canteen, the water so nearly hot it gagged him. He vomited the first mouthful, took a smaller sip and kept that down. Then, one-handed, he looped the rope around his waist and snubbed it close to the saddle horn so that if he passed out and fell the horse would drag him with it and someone might find them before he died. He paused only long enough to take Soto's horse with him.

Riding up the San Simon Valley, he held on to consciousness by cursing himself aloud. This was one of the very few times in his life when John Savage had been careless and that mistake could well kill him. He should have foreseen that Soto would fire a decoy shot to tempt him back, but the memory of Pete Slocum's behavior had tricked him into the folly of forgetting that Soto might act differently.

The sun went down and a full moon rose

and a cooler breeze against his clammy, sweated skin helped to keep him minimally alert. In the middle of the night the gray took him into Vic Tuker's ranch yard. The dogs set up a clamor, a lamp was lit and Tuker put his head out of an upper window.

"Who's down there? Sing out." The tone was suspicious.

The sheriff rode close beneath the window, afraid his weakened voice would not carry farther. "John Savage."

"Oh. Light down, Colonel. I'll have the pot boiling in a minute."

" 'Fraid I need a little help. Fast."

The dogs smelled the blood still seeping from the torn shoulder and were snarling, yapping, snapping around the gray's legs, jumping toward the rider. The horse danced, frightened, with sudden jerks. Savage clung to the horn to keep from falling where the brutes could sink their teeth into him. He nearly toppled before Tuker and his half-grown son ran through the door. The boy caught the rein and hauled the gray down while the rancher beat back the dogs, throwing rocks to drive them away. Savage untied himself and slipped into Tuker's uplifted arms, and with his good hand around Tuker's neck let himself be half-carried into the house.

The boy took the horses to the corral while his father settled the sheriff in a home-built chair with leather seat and back, then brought a tumbler half filled with whiskey cut with cool water, holding it to Savage's lips when the sheriff's hand trembled too much to lift it himself. Savage took it all in a single long swallow and the warmth eased the icy quaking of his stomach, then he sagged against the leather. Tuker, a widower, went for clothes and warm water from the stove well, peeled off Savage's vest and cut away the sodden shirt.

Bathing the caked and seeping blood from the wound, the rancher uncovered a long groove of ragged flesh and pronounced, "She went clean through and out. Now if she didn't chip a bone or leave a scrap of dirty shirt inside you ought to heal up all right."

He laid a poultice of homemade ointment over the gash and bound it with strips of old toweling, then held another fiery tumbler while Savage drank. As weak as he was, after the second drink the sheriff lost consciousness.

He did not know when Tim Tuker came and was sent to harness their team to the road wagon, make a thick bed of horse blankets, bring it to the door, then help to carry Savage out and lay him in the bed. They started for Tombstone immediately, Tim driving, Tuker sitting beside Savage, the gray and Soto's horse tied to the rear. Tuker took water and when the sheriff waked, feverish and dehydrated, poured sips into his mouth and bathed his face.

Vic Tuker knew the horse with four white stockings because Juan Soto had been in the San Simon Valley these last months. In this country men did not ask questions that might be considered prying, but since this was the sheriff who had been shot the rancher took the risk of rebuff.

"What happened between you and the Mexican, Colonel?"

Savage answered without hesitation. "I was a damn fool." It was more than he normally would admit to anyone, but the man had earned, was earning, the right to honest answers.

The road wagon had no springs and jolted viciously over the hardened ruts of the trail, and in spite of the pile of blankets he lay on, John Savage's shoulder was pounded unmercifully. He floated in and out of consciousness, jarred awake by pain every time the wheels dropped into a hole or hitched over a high spot. They were still ten miles from town at noon and in the hot sun the sheriff's fever parched his skin. Vic Tuker was kept busy dampening it and feeding him water. He was worried by the time Tim drove along Allen and stopped in front of Doc Combs' office, worried particularly that the doctor would be away visiting someone at a distant ranch.

But he was there and gave his stretcher to the ranch boy to carry to the wagon, then dragooned two men on the street to help shift Savage from the blankets and carry him indoors. He climbed into the wagon to make his examination, approved Tuker's ministrations and had the patient taken upstairs to his extra bedroom. When Savage was laid on the bed the doctor sent Tim Tuker for Edna Savage. She arrived with Old Sam on her heels, white-faced but composed as she looked down on her unconscious husband.

"How bad is the wound, Doc? Will he lose the arm?"

Combs was casual, his drawl slow. "I don't think he will unless complications set in. He'll have it rough for a while but as nearly as I can tell the flesh is clean and no bone is involved. It will take time to heal but this is one tough old rooster. I want him here where I can watch him until I'm sure there's no infection. Several days."

Tough as Savage was, he spent a week in Combs' bed before the doctor would let him out. Edna moved into the room with him to sleep beside him and nurse him. Sam posted himself at the foot of the stairs to make sure no enemy sneaked up to further harm the sheriff and Combs spelled him when he could. On his own Bobby Burch took word of the shooting to the Lazy S and both Bo Roberts and Mario Valdez rode back to Tombstone with him. The foreman assured himself that the Colonel would mend and returned to the ranch but Mario stayed.

"You can't keep watch day and night," he told Sam, "and the Doc has to make calls out of town. I'll take over at night."

The black man's voice was hostile. "I ain't forgot how you walked out on the Colonel and we don't need you now." He got out of the chair at the side of the steps and blocked the stairway.

Valdez sat down in the chair and laid his shotgun across his lap. "Sam, you old fool, I'm back at the ranch. Get the chip off your shoulder. Go get yourself some supper and bring me something when you've eaten. I said I'd take the night watch."

"I guess . . ."

Sam admitted to himself that he could not

keep awake day and night for long and was afraid he might fall asleep and let someone slip past him, and at least Mario could be trusted. He left the building, walking toward the Savage house. Four times he was stopped by businessmen who came out of their stores to ask anxiously after the sheriff's condition, was stopped by other passers-by. The show of concern and apparent popularity surprised the black rider. His opinion had been that the townies were only using the Colonel, wanting the protection he gave them but not appreciating what he was doing or liking him. On his return with a basket of food for Mario he was held up again and again by others asking about Savage.

"You know something," he told Valdez as he ate, in a tone of discovery, "I figured this town was just leaning on the Colonel for selfish interests, but everybody I passed wanted to know how he is like they really cared. Maybe I was wrong."

Mario swallowed his mouthful, tilting his head to one side. "I won't go that far. They've let him down every time he's needed them and they will again if anything more happens. Just watch."

Chapter 16

On the day Combs let Savage out of bed he took off the bandage, prodded at the swollen flesh around the wound, which was still angry red and raw, spread burning ointment on fresh cloth and covered the long gash again, hung the arm in a sling and bound it tightly against the sheriff's side.

"So you won't get frisky and tear out the stitches," he explained. "And if you want to use that wing again you do what I tell you. You've got the lid clamped on this town good, so Bobby Burch can handle it for a while. Go out to the ranch, take a rig. I don't want you on a horse until you're knit solid, a fall before then would cripple you permanently. Take it easy for a few weeks and I'll stop by when the sewing is ready to pull out. And John, if you don't follow orders, don't come to me again. Miss Edna, you sit on him."

Edna was there with clean clothes to help

dress her husband, to pull on his trousers, work his feet into the boots and button a shirt too large for him over the immobilized arm, her smile wide on the doctor.

"I'll use a bull whip on him if he takes one step out of line, Doc. Going home is the one good thing to come out of this business. I'll go have Sam bring the buggy."

She had turned to the door when Savage stopped her, saying, "First strap my gun belt on."

As she buckled it around his waist Combs grunted in scorn. "Don't you ever move without that thing on your hip?"

"I feel naked without it and I just could need it."

Savage settled the belt into a comfortable hang and sat on the edge of the bed, weak from the injury and the days of lying flat, while Edna went to take Sam to the house and prepare for the move. Both the black rider and Valdez kissed her when she told them of Combs' orders and Mario fidgeted impatiently at his guard post through the hour until the buggy drew up.

The drive to the ranch was festive. John Savage found it a big relief to be home. It was good to have Bo Roberts to talk with, good to see the crew and watch them at the chores. It was autumn but the weather was still very warm; the afternoon downdraft that usually cooled the house did not blow in this doldrum period. Day after day the sheriff rocked in his chair in the shade of the trot, fretting over his idleness.

Combs rode out, removed the stitches and said the shoulder was healing well and would mend all right, but Savage had doubts, feeling little improvement.

Three times the weekly Tombstone paper was brought out and Savage studied the issues attentively, judging the temper of the town. The reports were mostly of quiet, disturbed only by a few arrests for public drunkenness and two fights. In the second of those a Mexican was knifed in a row over a monte game but there was no other violence.

Savage finished the third paper and passed it to his wife across the parlor table where she crocheted by lamplight.

"Maybe we did get rid of the bad element, girl. If it stays this way I'll soon be able to turn the damned star over to Burch and go back to living."

Edna rose to come around the table and kiss his forehead. "Say that again and keep saying it. I haven't felt we were living since you put on that badge. It's been a nightmare. How soon do you think you can resign?"

He said evasively, "I'll go in and straighten out details as soon as I'm healed more."

He did not tell her how worried he was about the left arm. It remained stiff and his fingers would not flex as he thought they should. Perhaps he should go east to one of the big hospitals in Chicago or Kansas City, but he would not mention that possibility until he had talked again with Doc Combs.

The day he took off the harness that had bound the arm against his ribs for a month was one for celebration. He used it to go to Tombstone. Sam drove him in the buggy. It galled Savage not to ride but Combs had threatened him against getting on a horse until he gave permission.

It was a fine autumn morning, no cloud in the enormous arch of sky and the crystal mountain air so clear that distant hills looked blue and near enough to reach. They turned onto Allen close to noon. Savage left Sam to unhitch the team at the O.K. Corral and walked toward Combs' office. To those on the street the sheriff looked recovered and he was stopped repeatedly by men and women commenting that it was good to see him here again and hoping he was staying.

Combs was the only doctor left in the county and spent more time out of town than in. Today a note was hung on the door saying he would be back by one o'clock. Savage returned to the corral, picked up Sam and they spent the hour eating dinner in a restaurant. Combs was in when the sheriff approached the office again.

The doctor looked tired. He had a whiskey glass on the desk and filled another for Savage, making a sour joke that he wished so many people weren't taking sick at the same time.

"Now get out of that shirt so I can look you over. How's it coming?"

"I came in for you to tell me that. It's stiff and my fingers are numb."

Savage hung his gun belt over a chair back, pulled the shirttails out of his trousers and shrugged out of the shirt. The doctor flexed the arm, watching Savage's eyes for sign of pain, rubbed at the fingers individually, then bent one far back, hard. Savage cried out sharply in surprise and hurt.

"Good." Combs seemed very relieved. "They're coming around fine. You'll be as good as new before you know it."

Savage massaged his knuckle. "I wasn't at all sure. When are you going to let me ride?"

"Now. That will get your hand back in shape faster."

Combs lifted the whiskey bottle invitingly

but the sheriff waved it away and left, the weight of fear that his hand was damaged permanently lifted from his mind. He went next to the sheriff's office to sound out Bobby Burch about his taking over when Savage resigned.

The deputy sat behind the desk, his fingers together in a steeple against his nostrils, frowning morosely at the wall. He heard Savage's step, looked toward the door and heaved a harsh sigh.

"Sheriff. It's good you're here. I was supposed to send for you but I been racking my brain how to break the news. I still don't know any easy way."

John Savage's stomach knotted with premonition. "Just spit it out. What's wrong?"

"The bank. It's short over twenty-five thousand dollars. The examiner from Prescott found the shortage this morning and that's only part of it." Burch's next words came in a rush as though to get them out before his nerve failed. "Your brother-in-law has disappeared."

Savage's heart sank. "Verne? Absconded? When?"

The deputy nodded, looking sick. "He didn't show up for work yesterday. Knew the examiner was coming and blew town with the funds."

Savage sank on a chair, his mind turning over the implications of this stupidity. He found it easy to believe that Verne, losing at gambling and not having his sister handy to bail him out, would have helped himself from the bank, but how did the young idiot think he could get away with it? He swore silently. How was he going to break the news to Edna that her beloved brother was a thief of such magnitude?

"Who knows about this?"

"The examiner and Simpson, of course, and probably Don Wallace, the cashier. I don't know of any others. Simpson warned me not to talk about it. He's afraid of a run on the bank if it gets out."

Savage's mouth twisted as if he tasted gall. This was all the miserable town needed, a run on the only remaining bank. Tombstone would die completely and never revive.

He said sourly, "The last thing I want to do is talk to Simpson but I guess there's no way out. You sit tight until I come back."

Savage tramped up Tough Nut Street and shoved through the bank door. Simpson was in his rear office with the Prescott examiner, his face angry red and his wattles shaking when Savage came in.

"About time you got here," he exploded. "I'd begun to think that fool Burch hadn't sent for you."

Savage did not correct him. He acknowledged the introduction to Wilson Prickle and took a chair against the wall. Simpson did not give him time to speak, pounding his desk with a fat fist and bellowing.

"Your damned brother-in-law just about wrecked me. Lit out with a saddlebag full of bank money and by now he's most likely lost himself in Mexico, laughing at me. What are you going to do about him? First, you'd better make up the loss yourself."

Savage had considered that choice on his way here. Twenty-five thousand would not break him but it would put a sizable dent in his finances. And he did not know any place where he could market enough cattle at a fair price to make up the cash. Since the collapse of the town he had only the Indian Agency and the railroad construction camps to rely on and they could not absorb so much beef within months. He explained, his voice cold.

"It would take a good deal of time."

"I haven't got time. I told Burch to keep his mouth shut but he won't for long, the blabbermouth he is, and as soon as word gets around there'll be a run. That will be the end of Tombstone and it's your family's fault. You going to just sit there like a lump?"

Savage looked to the examiner. "Perhaps the state could take over, or stand behind this bank until I can repay it."

Prickle had a small, steel-trap mouth. He opened it for a single word. "Impossible."

"Of course not." Simpson's tone called John Savage an ignoramus. He clenched a fist and shook it at the sheriff. "It's up to you to go after Verne Hannah and find him before he loses the money he stole over a card table. I should have fired him a long time ago for gambling, but I figured your wife was keeping him and you've been my biggest account these last three years. Now you've got that badge don't think you can weasel out of your responsibility because he's your woman's brother."

John Savage's hand twitched, lifting toward the star. He ached to rip it off his vest and stuff it down this pompous banker's throat. Then he reined his sudden rage. He could not quit under this cloud on his family. He would not be hounded out of office by anyone. He stood up, nodded vaguely at the examiner, ignored Horace Simpson and walked out of the bank.

He stood on the sidewalk debating where to start his search. Northern Mexico was wide and deep, if indeed his brother-in-law had gone south. He could as well have taken a train east to lose himself in some large city. Only one thing was certain, the fugitive needed a horse to get out of Tombstone and neither the boy nor his parents owned an animal.

John Savage began at the livery, asking whether Verne Hannah had rented or bought a mount recently. The hostler said no, he had not seen the man except at the bank two weeks ago, and he was conditioned by his years in this untamed town not to ask questions. Savage left the barn wondering if Verne had gotten a horse from a friend, but as he had held himself apart from most people so he had from the boy and he did not know who the friend might be. Further, he did not want to talk to more men than necessary, to cause curiosity that would lead to speculation and the run that Simpson feared.

He thought of the elder Hannahs, with whom Verne had lived, who might know if their son had been planning a trip, but the chance was too great that word of his inquiry would reach his wife and he hoped to keep this trouble from her as long as possible. Then where to look? The more he thought of it the more probable place was south of the border, the closest hiding area, from early days the haunt of all types of outlaws.

Returning to his office, Savage told Bobby Burch he was leaving town and did not know when he would be back, without elaborating, then he located Sam to drive back to the ranch.

Mario Valdez was in the lower pasture schooling a pair of colts, a drill Edna was fond of watching but today she was not there. Savage saddled the gray while Sam attended to the rig and rode to the split-pole fence, got down and beckoned the rider. Mario led the young horses forward. Since leaving town he had let his hair grow long again and looked more like himself.

"Doc letting you ride now?" He sounded as pleased as Savage had been. "What's new in Tombstone?"

"Bad news."

The sheriff's eyes ranged over the free-rolling, unspoiled acres, green and deep now from the rains, and he cursed himself silently for ever leaving here. He would like most to stay, to forget the mired town that had already cost him dear and was apt to cost much more if or when his wife had to learn of her brother's defection. Unless Verne Hannah and the bank money were found soon and returned to Tombstone, Savage knew he would be accused of protecting him. For his own self-respect he must do his utmost to locate his brother-in-law. But if he did bring in the boy he could not foretell how Edna would react, how much strain would be put on their marriage. Surely his wife would not defend the theft, but would she not resent the part her husband must play in performing this ugly duty?

Mario Valdez read the troubled face and lost the wide smile that welcomed the Colonel home. "You look like it's personal. Care to tell me about it?"

John Savage told Mario as much as he knew and his judgment that Verne had jumped the border, adding the importance of finding the fool before the money was thrown away. He had hardly finished when Mario understood why the Colonel, usually so reticent, was unburdening himself here.

"I'm Mexican and you think I can find him where a gringo couldn't?"

"That's the size of it." Savage sounded as near beaten as anyone had ever heard him. "I'll take Edna and Sam to town where I can keep my eyes open at this end. You go through the villages, the cantinas, see if an American stranger has been around with money. I think you'd turn him up in time but I don't know how much we have before the lid blows up. Luck, anyhow."

CHAPTER 17

Mario Valdez rode south with provisions for two weeks, after which he was to report back whether he had learned anything or not. Savage returned to the sheriff's office and sent Bobby Burch to listen to the saloon talk, but not a hint surfaced for four days. Then a possible break came from an unexpected quarter.

Sam came to the Colonel at the jail office, in itself extraordinary, for the black rider avoided both that place and the courthouse with continuing hostility to officers of the law. Savage saw him twice pass the window on the opposite side of the street, then when the deputy had begun his morning round Sam crossed and came in, closing the door. That he came at all set the sheriff worrying. He was already disquieted, sitting at the scarred desk with the weekly newspaper noting the growing frequency of tax sales that pointed up the slippage of the county's economy and seeing a total collapse if Horace Simpson's bank failed. His mood made him jump to the thought that something had happened at the town house, perhaps to his wife. His tightening hands wrinkled the paper as Sam came in.

"What's wrong, Sam?"

Sam looked more bewildered than upset over an accident. "I don't rightly know, Colonel, I can't find the sense of it. Two Mexicans been sneaking around talking to Miss Edna and when I get near they all clam up until I leave. Like they was plotting a revolution or something."

A rush of relief made Savage want to laugh, but he choked it back. Edna Hannah Savage was too open a person to plot anything in secret. Still, he had a high regard for the shrewdness Sam had often proved and he waved at a chair.

"Sit down and start over at the beginning. When did you first notice these visits?"

Sam sat and shied his weathered straw hat onto the desk. "Day after we come back here."

The words jarred the sheriff. Three days. For three days something had been going on that he had no inkling of. He and Edna had always discussed everything that touched them without hesitation. What could be so private that she would exclude him from the knowledge? It leaped to his mind that she knew about her brother's theft and disappearance, but even so he would have staked the Lazy S that she would have come to him. There must be something else. The sudden ice inside him turned his voice cold.

"Is that all, Sam?"

The rider took the tone as accusation against him and he said hurriedly, "Colonel, you know I don't go spying on people, especially Miss Edna. I mind my own business unless I figure she's in some sort of trouble."

"What trouble?"

Sam clamped his knees with his hands, the large chocolate eyes worried. "I sure don't know, Colonel, but this morning she got that money box she keeps in the bank and brought it to the house. Those Mex went in the back way, then went out with a sack. I can't swear it but I think they had that box in the sack. Do you know what it means?"

The sheriff moved his head sideways slowly. The more Sam said the more confused the picture became. If Edna knew that Verne had stolen twenty-five thousand from the bank and intended to repay what she could from whatever she had saved, why had she not given the box to Simpson? Why take it from the safe and give it to two strange Mexicans?

Unconsciously Savage rubbed at his thigh with his blunt fingers. The straightforward move would be to go to his wife and ask her. It was a temptation. John Savage had never liked mysteries and liked deviousness less. But he did not want to appear not to trust the woman who had never done a disloyal act. It occurred to him that this was blackmail, that the Mexicans knew where her brother was hiding and were demanding money not to expose him. That she was paying them. Whatever, it made an ugly picture. When he had accepted the sheriff job he had not imagined it would put him into conflict with his wife. He brought his attention back to Sam.

"You wouldn't know where these men are now?"

"Yes I do. I followed them to the Marguerita Cantina on Allen Street in the barrio."

The tightness in John Savage loosened like a spring released. There was action to take. "Let's go." He stood up, easing the pearl-handled gun in the holster to be sure it was free, and preceded Sam out to the street.

The cantina was the last establishment of its kind in Tombstone. When they reached it Sam made to turn in but Savage stopped him with a touch on the shoulder and took him across the dust ribbon to an abandoned building with a dirty front window that faced the Marguerita entrance. They waited inside there.

It was a long hour's wait. Fat autumn flies darted against them, sticky as resin. For a time Savage batted them away, then gave up and suffered them unless they crawled on his face. Life's teaching and a natural bent had given him patience and he stood at ease, his breathing slow and regular while men went in and out through the swinging doors. The black rider was more restless, impatient and increasingly suspecting that the pair they watched for had left before he brought the Colonel. But at last he murmured in satisfaction.

"There they come."

The first through the batwings was squat, dark-skinned, with an old knife scar puckering one cheek. He came with a hand on his holster, pausing to look both ways before he stepped clear. The man behind him was a good six feet tall, long, thin mandarin mustaches at his mouth corners and drooped, bony shoulders making him appear enormously sad. He carried a flour sack weighted at the bottom, the cloth bulging around an object the size and shape of a cigar box.

The Mexicans ignored the few people on the street. When they were a block away Savage sent Sam to see where they went next. Since they had been watchful coming out of the cantina the sheriff did not want to be discovered trailing them, and went on to his office. Sam was not long. They had gone to the livery, mounted horses that had been left saddled and were riding east out of town.

"They're not in any hurry." But Sam was. "We can catch up short of a mile if we hustle."

"Not yet." Savage spoke deliberately. "Let them go for now. That wind last night blew out what prints any traffic left on the road and I can pick up the tracks. You stay and look after Edna."

He read rebellion in the dark eyes. Sam had made the discovery of the furtive activity at the house and he wanted to help look for answers.

Savage added, "You had better know the probabilities, but don't advertise them. Verne has disappeared and so has twenty-five thousand of bank money. My guess is these Mexicans are blackmailing my wife to not tell where he is. I have to see if they'll lead me to him, and bring him back."

"Oh Lord, Colonel. Poor Miss Edna. She got worry enough about you wearing that star." Sam headed for the house at a jog.

Savage trailed him with long strides as far as the livery, found the hostler in his cubicle with a *Police Gazette* and asked casually, "Those two Mexicans who just rode out. You know anything about them?"

The man twitched the straw he was chewing to the corner of his lips. "The Roco brothers, Jose and Chico. From south of San Luis Pass somewhere."

"Are they in town often? I haven't seen them before."

"Couple of times a year they bring in a little gold, fill their snoots at the Marguerita, then clear out. They never made any trouble yet."

"Thanks."

Savage flipped him a dollar. He always gave the man a little above what he paid to keep his horse here when he asked for information. From the beginning he had also kept extra traveling gear at the barn, ready for a sudden need. He saddled the gray, added the blanket roll and saddlebags, rode the street looking for Bobby Burch and hailed him when he came out of a saloon, told him in a low tone:

"I'm going out of town for a while, I don't know how long. Get word to my wife that I don't have time to go home now."

If it were not for the reason behind this trip John Savage would have looked forward to leaving these depressing streets and pushing across the hills and valleys he loved. He always felt a lift riding through the sparsely settled openness with a vista to stretch his sight to the distant peaks on the horizon where it was still possible that a few bronco Apaches up there followed the speck of a horseman through hot, fierce eyes, willing to starve rather than come down to the reservations they hated. But today the weight of his errand overwhelmed his pleasure and he rode with his eyes on the trail.

Just beyond the last of the inhabited buildings the sheriff saw the twin hoofprints of the Roco brothers. They had begun to run their horses soon afterward and must be fully confident, for there was no attempt to hide their passage by riding through the grit and brush out of the road.

But farther out they surprised him. He had assumed they would use the old smugglers' trail through Skeleton Canyon. Instead they swung south toward Bisbee

217

Canyon. They crossed the border at Douglas, continued south to Aqua Prieta, then west to Villa Verde, Del Rio and Cananea.

At Cananea he lost the trace. From Aqua Prieta on it had been increasingly difficult to isolate them from the growing volume of traffic. Cananea was larger than most of the area villages and Savage pulled up short of it, studying the cluster of pastel-washed buildings through the heat waves that still this far south shimmered in the air. The church was at the center on the plaza, the government house opposite, a single-story adobe structure with a flat roof and three-foot-deep window and door casings.

Savage was uncertain how to proceed now. He spoke Spanish as fluently as a native, but he was not a native. Gringos here were no better liked than border Mexicans were in Arizona, and in these mountain towns American strangers were regarded with unresponsive suspicion. He would get few answers to questions.

His best source might be the padre, for the condition of the church indicated it was in current use. At least a priest would have some degree of education, but whether or not he could or would help was open to conjecture. All Savage knew to do was ask.

He walked the gray to the stone steps, got

down, climbed to the solid door in the deep recess of the arch, pulled the heavy panel outward and looked in. The interior was very dim. He stepped inside and waited until he could see. It was a very old building with hand-hewn beams blackened by age and candle smoke. The altar was plain, the floor cool stone, the rows of benches simple and the Madonna with Child a crude local carving garishly painted.

The padre rose from prayers at the foot of the altar and walked toward Savage, a younger, more emaciated man than the sheriff had anticipated, asking what help he might offer in unexpectedly cultured Spanish. In the same language Savage asked if there were strangers in the town.

The priest said there was one, a tall Mexican who had ridden in that morning and spent the day in the cantina. The timing was right, the sheriff could not be more than a few hours behind the men he pursued and they could have separated. He thanked the padre and went back to the street to find the cantina around the corner on a crooked alley. The sun was just down and strong magenta tinted the air, almost a solid substance engulfing the buildings.

A guitar, singing, laughter directed him to a low door in the middle of the block. The serape door curtain was hooked back and wisps of blue cheroot smoke seeped out and up the pink adobe wall. Savage paused just inside until he could make out the bulks in the small, dim room. A very fat Indian woman behind a short bar leaned on it, resting her great breasts on the wet rings that covered the surface. Chairs at four small tables were occupied by men with mugs of warm beer before them. The table nearest the entrance was empty and Savage sat down there to look over the faces he could see. There were only two tall figures. One, quartered to him, was not the sorrowful-looking man he had seen in Tombstone. The other, his back to the door, wore shoulder-length black hair with a bright woven band around it. John Savage started at recognizing Mario Valdez.

He dropped his hat on the table so that it would not shadow his face and called to the woman for two beers, loud enough to override the noises. She drew the mugs and brought them and Mario quietly rose and sauntered after her, jackknifing into the next chair where both he and Savage could watch the room, lifting his pottery mug in salute.

"You decide you don't trust me with the expense money? I've hit every hut from

Skeleton Canyon to here and not heard a whisper about any gambling gringo."

CHAPTER 18

John Savage held Valdez' black eyes, brooding. "There's more now than just Verne's disappearance. I think Edna is being blackmailed, that she gave money to two Mexicans. I trailed them this far and lost them."

Mario swallowed his drink, making a face at the taste. "There's got to be an old boot in that barrel. Do you know what they look like?"

"One short with a crescent-shaped knife scar on his left cheek. The other's six feet, face like a professional mourner. If they came through here it was this morning. Jose and Chico Roco."

Valdez' brows went up. "In your pocket, Colonel. Last evening I rode in on a little rancho south of Imuris about a mile, maybe twenty miles below here, and smelled chili like I haven't had since I left home. I bought a bowl from the squaw, then camped out in the brush for the night so I could get some more for breakfast. I was just leaving an hour after sunup when your pair rode up the lane, one of them toting a flour sack. My horse is in the shed down the alley. I'll bring it up."

It was too easy. John Savage felt a letdown. This kind of luck was strange to him, for his successes had been hard-earned. And as a dividend by the time he and Mario could reach the place it would be an hour when they should find the men asleep.

Pulling up in the dark yard of the rancho, they saw no light through the oiled paper that glazed the single front window. They dismounted, tied the horses to the soap tree around the corner of the small adobe and were starting toward the door when ribald singing from the lane stopped them. They stood in the shadow while two riders materialized in the starlight, weaving in their saddles, fresh from the Imuris cantina. Their animals plodded to the corral gate without guidance and the six-foot man fell out of the saddle, used the poles to pull himself up and fumbled clumsily at the draw bar. While he tugged at it his short partner sat rocking with laughter.

Neither was aware of Savage and Valdez drifting in behind them. Simultaneously Mario caught the mounted man's arm, yanked him to the ground, disarmed him as he lay stunned, prodded his gun against the thick neck, and the sheriff clipped the one at the gate behind his ear, dropping him. Savage took a gun from the holster and a knife from the boot sheath, and dragged the limp body to where Mario was hauling his catch up by the shirt collar. Savage slapped him hard enough to sober him a little.

"Who is in the house?"

The man hiccuped. "Only my woman, señor. We have no money for you to steal."

"We're not thieves, Roco. Call to her to make a light and open the door."

The man hesitated until Mario shook him, making his head waggle, then he shouted the orders. There was no answer but shortly a lamp glowed and a thread of light widened into a rectangle. John Savage cocked his revolver under the conscious prisoner's nose, the barrel shoving against the upper lip, and spoke low to Valdez.

"I'll watch these while you see if he's lying."

Mario drew his .45 and approached the opening where the squaw stood holding the lamp above her head, peering out impassively. He patted her plump shoulder and smiled broadly.

"Your chili was so good I brought a friend

to try it, but first show me that you are alone."

He took her arm and steered her through the small main room, then the curtained-off sleeping quarters and the kitchen shed. They were all empty. He took her back to the door and hailed Savage, who came through prodding the squat scar-faced Mexican, dragging the tall one. The woman glanced at both with less than affection, but beamed up at Mario, not accustomed to being complimented on anything she did. She backed against the wall to be out of the men's way and apparently to enjoy whatever show was coming.

Savage dropped the limp form on its face and slammed the standing man against the wall opposite the woman, Roco's back hitting the adobe hard.

"What were you doing in Tombstone?"

Roco stood dumb, glaring, his Indian eyes hot. The sheriff stepped away, his gun steady.

"Answer. Now."

Roco shrugged and spoke sullenly. "We had business there."

"Blackmail? What did you take from Mrs. Savage? Money? Why?"

The man spat between Savage's feet and said nothing. Abruptly the woman beckoned to Mario, bent and pulled a mud brick out of the wall, a thin slab that left a cavity behind it to which she pointed. Valdez reached in and drew out Edna Savage's money box, opened it and exposed the neat sheaf of bills. The woman glared across at the squat man.

"They went to sell a man to his sister alive. They have him here. Tell them, Jose."

Jose Roco cursed her while John Savage tried to make sense of what she had said. News of the bank robbery had not leaked out at the time he followed the brothers from Tombstone, so what motive did they have for taking and holding Verne Hannah? Was there no connection, could it be coincidence? Could they have seen him in Mexico, recognized him and, knowing the Savage family had more wealth than most in the county, kidnaped him for ransom? Then Roco quit swearing and, since the squaw had betrayed this much of the secret, began an urgent explanation to save his neck.

"Señor Sheriff, is that not better than if we had killed your wife's brother? That is what Chico wanted to do right away, what we were to be paid for. But I said the price was not as much as your wife would pay to save him, and I was right."

There was acid in the sheriff's tone. "Who hired you for the murder?"

"The banker, Simpson. He said Hannah was stealing from him and that you knew it and wouldn't arrest him so this was the only way to stop him. Instead we took good care of him. Tomorrow we were going to let him go and warn him to keep away from Tombstone so Simpson would not learn he was alive."

"Where is he now?"

"In the stable. I'll get a lantern and take you there."

It could be a trap. Chico had come to and Mario had tied him and was free to watch Jose. Savage turned him over to Mario.

"Not you, Roco. Your wife will show me."

She went willingly to the kitchen, took the lantern from a peg, lighted it and went ahead of Savage through the rear door to the mud shed that had no door. There were no horses inside, only some gear to be mended and a pallet of straw where Verne Hannah lay asleep. His wrists and ankles were tied together at his back tightly enough that he could not work free but not blocking the flow of blood. He waked when the light hit his eyes, looked up angrily, then recognized his brother-in-law and sighed deeply.

"Colonel. Thank God you're here. Cut me loose."

"You're not hurt, Verne? Why in hell did you rob the bank?"

"Rob . . . ? Hell no I did not. Who said I did?"

Savage took the lantern from the squaw, told her to take off the thongs and stood by while she worked at the knots. When she finished Hannah sat up, stretched his cramped legs and arms, massaging the joints. The sheriff put the lantern down, rubbed the ankles briskly while Verne took care of his wrists. Savage did not answer the boy's question in the shed. He helped him to his feet, wrapped an arm around his shoulder and held him as he hobbled to the house. Verne was able to stand alone when they reached the main room. The woman paused to leave the lantern and when she joined them he bowed over her hand, kissing it.

"Thank you, ma'am, for your kindness and your chili. I won't forget either."

Savage said, "Now that we're all here, how did you get into this pickle?"

Not yet strong on his feet, Hannah sat down, frowning. "I have no idea, John. Simpson told me the Roco brothers were overdue to pay back a three-hundred-dollar loan and sent me here to collect. He loaned me a horse for the trip. As soon as I rode into the yard they threw down on me and tied me in that damn shed. I haven't seen them again until now. I heard them threaten this woman with a skinning if she let me escape, but none of them said a word to me. That's everything I know. What's it about?"

The Roco brothers were silent, wary as animals, their attention close on Savage. The pieces of the puzzle had fallen into place for him with Verne's story and he used Spanish so the helpful Mexican woman would understand.

"I went to Tombstone to see Doc Combs and Bobby Burch. Burch told me the bank examiner found the safe twenty-five thousand short and that you had disappeared. Simpson raised hell with me, insisted you had absconded and probably jumped the border. I see now it was an act to cover for taking that money himself. He made one mistake, hired the Rocos to murder you and hide your body but he was too cheap. They grabbed you all right but then they went to Edna and she gave them all the cash she had to turn you loose. You can thank Jose here for being greedy enough to double-cross Simpson."

He moved to plant himself in front of the Rocos. "What did you tell my wife about her brother?"

Jose, eager now to co-operate, crossed himself. "A part of the truth, Sheriff, that we were holding him for a ransom. Also we said he had won all our money by cheating in a card game and all we wanted was to get it back."

The sheriff grunted. So that was why Edna had said nothing to him. If she believed Verne guilty of crooked gambling she would certainly rather pay for his release and then face him with the charge herself than admit how wrongly she had defended her favorite for so long. He waggled a forefinger between the pair.

"Can either of you write?" When both nodded he continued. "I want your confession down on paper. Tell your wife to bring materials and I'll dictate to you, Jose."

When she laid a torn square of brown wrapping paper, a quill and inkwell before him Roco dipped the quill, apologizing:

"I can only write in Spanish, señor. Will that do?"

"That will do," Savage told him. "Begin with this. I, Jose Roco, and my brother, Chico, were hired by Horace Simpson in Tombstone, Arizona, to kidnap and kill

Verne Hannah, his employee."

When that was written readably he continued dictating what Jose had said they had done, watched the man sign his name, asked Mario to untie Chico so he could add his signature, had Mario witness the paper, then told him:

"Go see if Simpson's horse is in the corral. If it is, saddle it and move ours over with the Rocos'." When Valdez had gone Savage said over his shoulder, "Verne, are you up to riding tonight?"

The boy laughed raggedly. "I'll tell you when I try. I'll do my best."

The sheriff folded and pocketed the confession, for the first time feeling some respect for his wife's brother. Jose Roco pointed at Edna's money box, which lay open on the table, and wheedled:

"Sheriff, I saved his life. Shouldn't I have a reward?"

Savage looked into the box, judging that there was no more than three hundred dollars in it, and nodded. "I suppose you earned it, you and your wife."

The man exulted to his brother, "You see how it pays to do a good thing. And you would have killed for Simpson's measly fifty pesos." He pounced for the box but Savage shoved it out of reach.

"We'll leave it with her. You two are going to Tombstone to testify."

"No. No." Both brothers shouted it and Jose went on, "I don't want to go up there where he can shoot me. You have the paper, isn't that enough?"

It would be, Savage thought, in a court of any integrity, but in Malcomb's or Ben South's hearings he needed the most evidence he could bring before them. He would call the bank examiner from Prescott to disclose that twenty-five thousand dollars were missing and, coupled with the Rocos' story, there should be evidence enough to raise a cry against the banker that not even Tucson could squelch. If it closed the bank and finally finished Tombstone that would have to be. He had tolerated much, worked hard against odds, but blackening his brother-in-law's name and trying to have him murdered was more than too much.

When Mario had the horses ready he and Verne bound the Roco men and tied them in their saddles, put each on a lead rope, then they and the sheriff mounted and started north. They passed through silent little Imuris, rode five miles farther and camped to sleep for what was left of the night.

CHAPTER 19

John Savage was particularly watchful on the way to the border. He was leading two prisoners whom he had no legal right to have arrested in Mexico. He had no authority in the neighbor country and did not want to run into a patrol there. Such trivia as legalities had never stopped him from taking what actions he found necessary, for in the frontier West a strong man made and lived by his own law.

A group of horsemen appeared far ahead riding toward them. Savage took his party off the road and out of sight, warned the Rocos to stay quiet, left Mario and Verne to enforce the order with drawn guns, dismounted and went back to where he could see who passed. They were a band of Rurales, heavily armed and in a hurry, but none of them looked his way. When they were well gone he resumed his trek.

Cold anger rode like a cannon ball in his

gut. He was sorely tempted to pick up banker Simpson and drag him to Skeleton Canyon, but that would not really satisfy him. What he wanted more than a quick, easy death for the man was a long retribution, to see him in the hellhole of Yuma prison for the rest of his life with the most vicious outlaws for company; yet the Tucson Ring might block him once again. He had to find some other solution and as he rode he thought it through.

They camped another night outside Aqua Prieta and just at noon came to drowsing Tombstone. The sheriff led his small caravan toward the head of Allen Street at an easy walk.

Mario Valdez kicked his mount up beside the sheriff, protesting, "Colonel, Simpson's sure to see Verne and the Rocos if you go in this way and he'll probably bolt."

"Just what I want. Flush him into the open. Even with the confession and testimony I'm afraid Tucson will butt its nose in and I'll lose the case again. Now, Simpson hasn't been out of town for months so he has that money somewhere here, and if he packs it and runs it will prove his thievery to the town when I pick him up."

Mario had his doubts but the sheriff was too often right to argue with and he said nothing. Savage stopped the column and moved back to the other men.

"We're going straight down Allen," he told them. "I want you Rocos seen. At the jail, Verne, the Rocos and I will go inside while Mario takes the horses around to the back. Verne, you'll take Jose and Chico on through and mount them again, leave my gray, use the alley to the town house, pick up your sister and Sam and high-tail it to the ranch where you're out of reach in case the word that you robbed the bank has gotten out. I'll watch for Simpson to make his jump and nail him."

They rode on, passing the Alhambra saloon. Habitually banker Simpson closed his door at twelve and stopped for two drinks at the bar on his way home to dinner. He was almost certain to be there now.

At the office Bobby Burch looked up from the desk and narrowed his eyes at the sight of Verne Hannah.

"So you found him, Sheriff. Did you get the money?"

"He didn't take it. Simpson himself did." Savage paused where he could watch the saloon door as the other three went on. "You chase up to the Alhambra, use the rear door and if Simpson comes out follow him, then come tell me where he goes. On the double." The deputy wanted to ask questions but Savage said sharply, "Jump."

Burch jumped. Savage waited, expecting at any moment to see the banker hurry to the street and hotfoot it toward his house, where he thought the money would be hidden. But Simpson did not appear. Within minutes though Bobby Burch was back, running, panting as he came in, stammering.

"He didn't leave and hell's busting loose. How come you brought those men down here like a parade?"

"For Simpson's reaction, to make him grab the money he stole and run. Did you see him?"

"He's reacting all right but not that way. He's in there yelling that Verne Hannah embezzled twenty-five thousand and took off with the two Mexicans you brought in with him. If he runs it will be this way. He's saying he doesn't think you're in on the theft but why wasn't Verne tied like the other pair unless you're covering him because he's family. And he's buying drinks all around, sending men to spread the word, working up a necktie party, saying they'll have to come here and take Verne out whether you like it or not. Where is Hannah now? And how do you know he isn't guilty?"

Savage handed Burch the confession and when he had read it said, "They're all on the way to the ranch. Valdez will hold the Rocos there in case I need them. Looks like you and I may have to stand off a siege."

"Oh no. Not me. That crowd will be drunk in ten minutes and all their money was in that bank. They want a hanging and if they can't get at Verne they'll lynch anybody who's in this office. I just resigned."

The deputy bounced his badge on the scarred desk and went hurriedly through the rear door. Savage followed him to lock up, then went to the gun rack, loaded all four shotguns and lined them up on the desk, then stood at the window watching a mob grow before the Alhambra. Within fifteen minutes it seemed that every man in town was there and an ominous growling and shouting rose louder each passing second.

It was stupid to stay there, Savage decided. If they broke in there would be a carnage to no purpose. He had better leave while he could. Going again to the rear door, he unlocked it and pulled it inward, looking for the gray. The horse was not there and as he put his head out to see along the alley a series of .45 shots drove him back though no one was in sight.

So he was bottled up. It made him mad, mad at the town but madder at himself for thinking of retreat. He changed his tactic again. If he were going to die here it was not going to be hiding behind the flimsy front wall. By the time he reached the desk once more the mob was moving, less than a block away. Taking a shotgun and filling his pockets with shells, he stepped out to the street and stood waiting in the dust.

You could not reason with a crowd of enraged drunks with hanging on their frozen minds. He fired both barrels over the approaching heads, reloaded and emptied both chambers again in front of their feet. The front line stopped but the surging rank behind forced them on. Savage looked for Simpson and located him at the rear fringe egging on the mob at the top of his voice. If the sheriff could get a clear shot at him he would willingly blow him apart, but he did not want to kill others if he could help it and the banker was surrounded.

One of the men in front being reluctantly shoved forward shouted, "Don't shoot again, Sheriff, it ain't you we're after. We want that damn brother-in-law and we mean to have him."

Savage called, "He isn't here. Turn around before somebody gets shot. It's Horace

Simpson who took that money. I have proof."

There was ragged, sarcastic laughter and another shout. "That's crazy. It's his own bank. You can't save Hannah's neck with a lie like that. Boys, maybe we do want the sheriff too."

Without warning a noose sailed out, thrown from the roof over the sidewalk behind Savage. It dropped over his shoulders to his elbows and was pulled tight, yanking his arms against his sides so suddenly that he lost his grip on the shotgun, let it fall. He reached for his holster but the man on the roof jerked the rope, pulled him off his feet. He landed on his side, the holster beneath him, and before he could roll to reach the pearl-handled gun they were on him. A boot ground his hand into the dirt and another kicked his holster empty. His wrists were lashed behind his back and he was grappled to his feet, tightly held.

Now Simpson came forward to take control. John Savage had to die while the mob still believed Verne Hannah was guilty, before the sheriff could produce the Roco brothers to expose the banker. His voice raised near hysteria, Simpson led the lynchers to the O.K. barn where a beam extended from the gable above the hay loft with a pulley for hoisting bales of feed to the upper door.

Savage did not fight the pushing and pulling hands. He saw no hope of rescue with all his people on their way to the Lazy S, and neither Lew Trumble nor the bartender Joel Morrison was in the crowd. He stood rigidly beneath the pulley while the noose that pinioned his arms was wrenched up about his neck, the free end of the rope flung up through the mow door. A horse without a saddle was brought from the barn and he was boosted onto the bare back, his arms tied behind him, and was held as someone climbed the inside ladder, tossed the rope over the beam, snubbed it short and began knotting it. When it was secure and taut Savage knew that Simpson would strike the horse. It would jump away and drop him. Either his neck would snap or he would hang strangling until he choked. He sat straight, unmoving, his face quiet, his eyes hard, cold, focused over the heads of the men who jeered up at him. These men for whom he had given so much effort to make their town safe.

Savage had been close to death many times but never closer than he was at this moment. His mind reviewed the happenings of the past. He wondered who would take care of the ranch, of his wife. Certainly her family had never shown any talent for either responsibility.

Abruptly there came new sound, new shouting from the side, and Savage shifted his eyes toward it. To his astonishment a mounted group appeared, driving hard around the corner of the corral at the flank of the mob. Lew Trumble led them with Jay Osborne close behind, then Doc Combs and Henry Malcomb and Joel Morrison. Trumble rode with his reins between his teeth, both hands firing heavy guns into the air for attention. It looked as though the man who had first come up the trail beside him had belatedly been able to rouse the core of solid citizens to take action of their own.

Trumble's horse knocked a man from his feet and the crowd began giving way as the other riders rode down on them. That was as much as John Savage saw. With a yell of outrage Simpson flung a balled fist against the animal Savage straddled. It bolted into the barn runway and the sheriff was dragged off its rear to fall and hang twirling a foot short of the ground.

His neck did not break but the noose tightened around his larynx, cutting off breath. With his wrists bound behind him he could not loosen it. Red color flamed through his brain and burned against the backs of his eyes. He corded his throat against the biting rope, drew in a seep of air but it was not enough. He was losing consciousness when unseen hands closed around his knees, lifting him, others cut the rope and fought the noose over his head. He gasped in life as he was laid on the dust and for a while could only hear.

Lew Trumble's bellow: "Damn you, Simpson. Damn you to hell."

The banker's sputtered yelp: "They robbed the bank. They robbed the bank." The words came in spasms, as though the breath was being shaken out of him.

John Savage fought to clear his vision, opened his eyes and through the red haze made out Trumble, both hands around the banker's throat worrying him like a dog with a rat.

Other feelings and sights came slowly into focus. His wrists being cut free, hands helping him to sit up, a gun being placed in his palm and his fingers closed around the butt. Joel Morrison's voice, laughing, telling him:

"Use it on Simpson if you want. I wouldn't blame you."

Savage blinked about him. By now he was

surrounded by mounted men, all with arms drawn, men who were crowding the mob back and they were giving way rapidly. It was one thing to attack the unarmed sheriff, quite another to face this roused and bristling band. With the strength of iron will the sheriff forced himself slowly to his feet and stood swaying, his legs braced apart for balance, batting away the hands that would have supported him.

As control returned he stepped to where Lew Trumble still had a vise grip on a pale and shaking Simpson, nodded to the rider to let go, put the barrel of the gun against the back of the banker's neck and prodded him up the street, the riders escorting them in a triumphant parade to the jail. Silent, Savage walked the banker into a cell, locked him there and left, ignoring Simpson's blustering threats against every man who had taken part in the rescue, promising that as soon as he could get word to Tucson they would all be in grave trouble.

Some of the band had dismounted and trailed into the jail, others had remained mounted and on guard in the street, but the mob had dispersed and scattered out of sight. When Savage returned outside he found that a sobered, angry Hal Hawser, the county attorney, had arrived and learned of the attempted lynching from Lew Trumble. Savage interrupted their talk, showed Hawser the Roco confession, asked Trumble to ride to the Lazy S and bring the brothers to town, and when he had gone took Hawser to the cell to try to make the banker talk.

But Simpson had quickly recovered his poise and when Savage asked about the stolen money he jeered at them.

"Find it if you can. You have no shred of proof of this ridiculous accusation. What's the worth in the words of a pair of starving Mexican border bums as against mine? You'll soon find out which the territorial authorities will believe."

"He's right on that," Hal Hawser grumbled when they had retreated to the sheriff's office. "Unless we can find that money in his possession we haven't the ghost of a case."

John Savage found only a frustrated sigh in answer. Time and again he had watched the courts turn offenders loose almost before he booked them. Hawser went off, shaking his head in helplessness, and the sheriff sent out for coffee, then sat over it at his desk, brooding. He had never wanted this job. He had done his best to save this dying town and now to be forced to sit here and see Simpson too go scot-free was too much to bear. The only bright spot in the bleak prospect was that at last some men at least had risen to face down the hooligans themselves. It was little enough accomplishment with which to leave the office.

It was after midnight and Savage still sat when Lew Trumble returned with the Roco brothers. They did not come alone. Edna Savage rode with them ahead of Mario Valdez, Bo Roberts and the entire crew. The boys were spoiling for a fight and were bitterly disappointed that the mob had faded, that there was no action in sight. Savage ordered them all to go to the town house and stay there, not to visit any saloon. He had seen trouble enough for this day.

But neither Valdez nor Roberts would leave him. It was too likely to them that an attempt would be made to release the banker and they wanted to hear the story from the Colonel himself. They gathered around the desk as Savage concentrated on talking to his wife, telling all that had happened and what bleakness lay ahead, spreading his hands in uncharacteristic hopelessness.

"Hal Hawser says, and I know it's true, we'll never make a case against Simpson unless we can find that money and tie it to him. I wouldn't know where to start looking."

Mario Valdez began a deep, rumbling, growing chuckle. "I know exactly where he'd hide it. Right here in town. Come on, I'll show you." He spun toward the door but Savage stopped him.

"Hold on, Mario, we'll need Hal Hawser as witness. Bo, go find him, get him over here. He's probably in the Alhambra."

No one in the office spoke again as they waited. If Mario was wrong their last chance was gone. When the county attorney followed the foreman through the door his face wore the same doubt, but Mario was confident.

He led them in a group to the Simpson property, around the house and into the barn where the ornate carriage sat. He lighted a lantern, took a hammer and chisel from the workbench and climbed into the well below the driver's seat, reaching a hand down.

"Come up here, Colonel. Remember, I used to drive this rig. One day when Simpson didn't know I was around I saw him pry up this seat, put a package in the box and nail it shut again."

When Savage was beside him Mario drove the chisel under the board, drew three nails and lifted the seat, then stood back. The sheriff leaned down and pulled out a heavy sack, opened the draw string and dumped the contents at his feet. Sheaf after sheaf of banded bills tumbled quietly on the floorboards. Hal Hawser pressed forward with the lantern, riffled through the sheafs, dropping them one by one back in the sack, drew it closed, slung it over a shoulder and thumped Mario on his arm, his eyes hard and bright as Savage had never seen them.

"Good day's work, Valdez. This cinches it. We have a case that will stand up. And high time."

They walked back to the office, Mario and Bo with hands on their guns, watchful that no shape darted out of a dark alley to snatch at the precious evidence. Walking between Savage and Hawser, Edna crooked a hand under her husband's elbow and leaned against him, sounding tired and wistful.

"John, you have finished the worst job you ever tackled. Surely we can go home now?"

Hal Hawser cut in hastily. "Not quite, ma'am. I need him at Simpson's trial. And we need him in the office with a lot more than one deputy until that banker is out of this town and locked up in Yuma prison. I don't want to lose this one to a lynch mob."

John Savage squeezed his wife's hand

against his side and twisted a sardonic smile down on her.

"You wouldn't want to deny me the one single pleasure of seeing one arrest stand up in court, would you? But just as soon as I see that happen I'll beat you in a race to the Lazy S."

ABOUT THE AUTHOR

Todhunter Ballard is the author of more than fifty novels, including *The Californian, Package Deal, Nowhere Left to Run, Loco and the Wolf,* and *Home to Texas.* His book *Gold in California!* won the Spur Award of the Western Writers of America as the best historical novel of 1966. Mr. Ballard has also written numerous television scripts and short stories for virtually every national magazine. His most recent novel is *Trails of Rage.*

We hope you have enjoyed this Large Print book. Other Thorndike, Wheeler, and Chivers Press Large Print books are available at your library or directly from the publishers.

For information about current and upcoming titles, please call or write, without obligation, to:

Publisher
Thorndike Press
295 Kennedy Memorial Drive
Waterville, ME 04901
Tel. (800) 223-1244

or visit our Web site at:

www.gale.com/thorndike
www.gale.com/wheeler

OR

Chivers Large Print
published by BBC Audiobooks Ltd
St James House, The Square
Lower Bristol Road
Bath BA2 3SB
England
Tel. +44(0) 800 136919
email: bbcaudiobooks@bbc.co.uk
www.bbcaudiobooks.co.uk

All our Large Print titles are designed for easy reading, and all our books are made to last.

Library Link Issues (For Staff Use Only)

KW

1	2	3	4	5	6	7	8	9
	288A					780A		